NORTH TO TEXAS

**Center Point
Large Print**

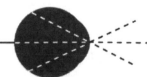

**This Large Print Book carries the
Seal of Approval of N.A.V.H.**

NORTH TO TEXAS

Noel M. Loomis

CENTER POINT PUBLISHING
THORNDIKE, MAINE

This Center Point Large Print edition
is published in the year 2010 by arrangement with
Golden West Literary Agency.

The text of this Large Print edition is unabridged.
In other aspects, this book may vary
from the original edition.
Printed in the United States of America
on permanent paper.
Set in 16-point Times New Roman type.

ISBN: 978-1-60285-706-3

Library of Congress Cataloging-in-Publication Data

Loomis, Noel M., 1905-1969.
North to Texas / Noel M. Loomis. -- Large print ed.
p. cm.
ISBN 978-1-60285-706-3 (library binding : alk. paper)
1. Texas--History--Civil War, 1861-1865--Fiction. 2. Large type books. I. Title.
PS3523.O554N67 2010
813'.54--dc22
2009043373

To Mary and Gary
They are the most.

PREFACE

POSSIBLY the only Civil War land battle fought on Texas soil before Lee surrendered was the Battle of the Nueces, in which a force of sixty-five Unionists, trying to escape from Texas into Mexico, were caught by Confederate troops and, to put it bluntly, massacred. Captain C. D. McRae of the Second Texas Mounted Rifles was in command of the Confederate force, but a Scotch professional soldier, Captain James Duff, gets a large share of blame for the shooting and hanging of nine wounded men who surrendered.

No man survived who fell into Confederate hands on the Nueces that day. Six who escaped during the battle were later killed crossing the Rio Grande. Others who escaped made their way into Mexico, and many of these served in the Union army during the war.

The Battle of the Nueces points up the lack of unanimity among citizens of Texas over the entire question. The vote on secession was divided, some whole counties going against it. The feeling against war with the Union was even stronger, for few persons in Texas had believed that secession would bring on a war. Then too, Sam Houston did not favor the war, and his word carried power in the state of Texas.

For a short time all of Texas was under martial

law, but this was soon relaxed. At various times in succeeding months, however, different counties were declared in open rebellion against the Confederacy and subjected to military rule. For a long time conscription in Texas was not successful because of native opposition, which was strongest around San Antonio and up near the Red River.

To complicate matters, Texas was a vital area to the Confederacy, for, with the Union blockade in effect, Texas was the back door to Mexico, and across the Rio Grande was smuggled a large portion of the matériel so desperately needed by the South—firearms, textiles, ammunition, and medicine. On top of all this, the behavior of Confederate troops (as opposed to native Texas "guards") was not always gentlemanly, and feeling between Confederates and Unionists in some parts of the state was intense. It is said there were 171 Unionists hanged in Cooke County alone at the height of the trouble—thirty-two on one tree. Some of these hangings were legal but of dubious justification; others were lynchings.

As for the background of espionage in the story, Harnett T. Kane, in *Spies for the Blue and Gray*, says "this war probably saw more espionage than any in our history." The Civil War became "a spy-conscious war, and sometimes it seemed that everybody was spying on everybody else and talking volubly on the subject, in newspapers, parlors, bars and at street corners."

This story of the quinine runners attempts to give a picture of one aspect of all this conflict and confusion. There are a good many historical characters, including all those at the Battle of the Nueces except Roy Talley and his two brothers. The battle itself is told in accordance with facts as related by John Sansom, who was there as represented.

Men like A. J. Hamilton (who became a Union general and later was appointed provisional governor of Texas) appear briefly. Most of the fictional characters are adapted from men and women who played parts on the stage of Texas history. Sam Houston's speeches, while not delivered in the town of Austin, are a matter of record. The arson of houses, hiding out along the Colorado River, burnings in effigy, and fleeing to Mexico, were not uncommon in those turbulent days. Nor was smuggling, profiteering, or outlawry. Nor were malaria and the urgent need for quinine in a South fighting with its back to the wall.

NOEL M. LOOMIS

August 25, 1955

CHAPTER I

ROY TALLEY had hung over the side of the chute all day. The black Louisiana dirt, pulverized by thousands of flinty hooves, rose in heavy clouds. It billowed slowly in the still air, and settled back down on the hats and skin and clothing of the men at the chutes. But Roy Talley was interested in only one thing: cows. His arms hung over the top edge of the rough cypress plank. His hands, under the gray film of dust, showed knuckles cracked open from cold and water. His gray-blue eyes searched out the brand on every cow as it went through, and the totals mounted in his head.

He watched the last heifer scat into the quarter-master's holding herd, helped by a resounding smack over the rump, and stepped down. He was not a big man—about five-feet-eight—and not heavy, but rather small-boned and solidly put together.

He glanced at the herds spread out over the grass. The Confederate army indeed must have needed beef, for they had sorted the stuff as fast as it had come through the chute. Probably tomorrow they would be moving the animals off toward Virginia. Well, his job was finished as far as the cows were concerned; all he had to worry about now was getting the money back home to Texas.

He turned to the man in butternut brown at his side. "You get that Quién Sabe steer about fifteen head back?" he asked.

The sergeant looked up through the dust. "Fancy Spanish brand, you mean?"

"Yeah."

The sergeant wet his forefinger and flipped a page of his small black notebook. Talley glanced at the entry: "Steer. 6 yrs. '?' on left hip."

Talley nodded. The sergeant closed his notebook, and Talley turned as a gray-uniformed officer came up, slapping the calf of his leg with a riding whip. "You're a good trailman, Mr. Talley. This is the best beef I've seen in six months."

"Longhorns rustle for themselves," said Talley. "Long as we can keep the Comanches away we're all right."

Captain Robertson seemed well-pleased. "This stuff will be a lifesaver to General Beauregard— and I will see that you are favorably mentioned in my report to the quartermaster general."

Talley looked over the Confederate captain's shoulder, at the men on horseback cutting out cattle and hazing them through clouds of dust so thick it obscured the waters of Lake Pontchartrain. The bawling of cows, the frightened bleat of lost calves, and the never-ending "Hooya, hooya!" of the cowhands brought no emotion through the layer of fine gray dust on his face as he turned back to Robertson. "I did not bring these cows here for a kind word from the Confederate War Department, Captain. I brought them here for money."

Robertson looked at him sharply. "The Confederacy is not asking donations, Mr. Talley. We will pay the price agreed on."

Talley nodded. "That's all I want."

Robertson made an obvious effort to be friendly. "Is this all your own stuff, Mr. Talley?"

"Everything with my road brand was gathered on our place. There's a few strays I'll have to account for when I get back home, but you may have noticed most of the brands are R Bar T."

"You must have a fair-sized piece of land back in Texas."

"Forty thousand acres up along the Colorado River above Austin."

"Was it your pa who went to Texas from Mississippi?"

"The same."

"Fought in the Texas Revolution?"

"Yes."

"I hear he did right well for himself."

"He had a Mexican grant before the republic. Afterwards made some good buys on land and had some good years—no bad drouth, no bad winters."

"I hear next to Sam Houston he carried as much weight as anybody in Texas."

Roy didn't answer.

Robertson obviously had more on his mind, but Talley gave him no encouragement. After a pause Robertson said, "It will take an hour or two for the sergeant to run up the totals. I see you didn't keep a record."

Talley looked at him. "I kept it in my head."

Perhaps Robertson wasn't accustomed to handling cattle; from his speech he was a Georgian. "By age and sex too, I suppose."

"By age and sex," said Talley.

Robertson smiled faintly. "How many six-year-old steers would you estimate in your two herds, Mr. Talley?"

Talley's blue-gray eyes fixed on the captain's face. "I wouldn't estimate, Cap'n. There are 1,341 six-year-olds in that outfit."

Robertson eyed him for an instant, then he looked at the sergeant. "We'll wait for your totals, Pierce."

Talley went to a post, flipped the reins of a *bayo naranjado* gelding from around it, and swung into the saddle. "His count better agree with mine," he said, and rode off.

He walked the orange-and-white horse through the streets of New Orleans. Some of them had been paved with stones since the previous time he had been there—three years before with his father—and occasionally the *bayo's* shoes struck fire from them.

He dismounted before the St. Charles Hotel,

with only a glance for its huge dome and its Corinthian portico. A Negro stableboy stepped out, and Talley gave him the reins.

"A rubdown, suh?"

"That horse would tear down the stable if you tried to rub him. Let him roll, and give him a quart of oats."

"Yas, suh."

Talley went inside. An ornate oil lamp with a painted shade hung over the clerk's desk. "Hot water in my room," said Talley. "Right away. I want a bath."

"Yes, *sir.*" The clerk jangled a hand bell.

Talley started up the broad stairway. Then he heard voices from the barroom, felt the need of something, turned back and went to the bar. "Bourbon," he said.

The bartender spun out a small glass and slid a large bottle next to it. Talley poured the glass full and dropped a silver half dollar on the bar.

He tossed down the whisky and poured another. He raised it and saw a gray-uniformed young man watching him. He finished the drink, set down the glass, and started for the lobby.

The young man met him at the door. "Aren't you the man who brought the beef from Texas?" he asked.

"Yes."

"Sir," said the young man, "I hope you will be good enough to have a drink with me."

Talley hesitated. "Since you put it that way—" He turned back to the bar a little reluctantly. He had no wish to drink, and far less to be drawn into an argument.

They were surrounded by the stranger's friends, and Talley noted a number of gray uniforms.

"I'm Claudio Dujet," said the young man.

Talley shook hands as he gave his name.

Dujet lifted his glass. "To that greatest of all military geniuses," he proclaimed. "General Stonewall Jackson."

Talley tossed down the drink. The young blades of New Orleans were murmuring around him.

"Another!" shouted Dujet, more than a little drunk.

Talley looked for a way out, but Dujet had him buttonholed. "To the greatest army in the world!" Dujet proclaimed. "The Army of Northern Virginia!"

Talley looked around him, remembering that he still had to get his money from Robertson. A gray-haired man, not tall but inclined to fatness, was drinking at the bar a few feet away. At that moment he raised his head and looked into Talley's eyes, and there seemed to be a message there. Talley lifted his glass and tossed down the drink, wondering where he had seen the fat man before.

Voices rose around him, but he spoke up: "I'll buy one. Then I'm going to get cleaned up."

"What's it to?" shouted Dujet.

Talley looked at the dark-eyed, dark-haired, typically volatile Creole. It wasn't a good spot. He had to avoid trouble. He glanced at the fat man and saw again that curious interest in his face. The fat man had just taken a blue bandanna out of his hip pocket, and now he raised it to his nose, but instead of blowing into it he brushed the tip of his nose three or four times and put the handkerchief back in his pocket. The gesture identified him for Talley; the man had been around the chute for the last two or three days; Talley had supposed him to be a Confederate official. Talley turned to his friends and raised his glass. "To Texas!" he said loudly.

"To Texas! To Texas!"

He finished his drink, shook hands with Dujet, thanked him, and managed to get out. He went through the luxuriously furnished lobby and started upstairs.

"Mr. Talley!" called the hotel clerk. "It will be a little while, sir, before your bath is ready. My man let the fire go out under the boiler. Very sorry, sir."

Talley stopped, annoyed. "How long?"

"Half an hour, sir. If you will have a seat—"

Talley nodded, suppressing his impatience. He stifled a yawn, closed his eyes, and rubbed his whiskered face with both hands. He started for a big leather chair in the corner of the lobby, but he saw Helen Partridge and changed his course to her direction.

She looked up as he approached. She was almost as tall as he, but bigger boned. Nevertheless she moved easily, and her black hair looked nice against a heavy red silk dress with a small white collar.

"Mind if I sit down?"

She nodded. "Glad to have some company." Her voice was low and rather musical. Her heavy mass of black hair gleamed as her head moved under the oil light. "These are long days."

"With no news from your husband?"

"Not since he sent word to meet him here."

He said, watching her, "Didn't you say you came to New Orleans six days ago, now?"

She glanced at him. "Yes, the day before you brought your cattle in."

"You came here from New York?"

"Yes—by ship."

He tried to make the words sound idle: "I thought the Federals were blocking the coast."

"Yes, of course—but we slipped into Biloxi about ten days ago." She smiled ruefully. "The Federals don't mind how many are coming into the Confederacy. It adds to the need for supplies—food, clothing, medicine."

After a pause, he said, "And your husband is in the Confederate army?"

"With the W. P. Lane Rangers."

"That's a Texas outfit."

"Yes."

"And has been stationed on the Texas frontier all during the war," he said, watching her.

"It is confused," she admitted. "Sam and I were married in Baltimore. Right afterward my father became ill in England, and I went over there. That was a year ago—April 1861. Sam didn't think there would be a war."

"Sam was wrong," he noted, "just the same as a lot of us were wrong in Texas."

"It has taken me all this time to get back," she said. "The British ships would not run the blockade."

"Yes, ma'am," said Talley, watching her intently. "But your husband, on duty with Lane's men, stationed in West Texas—and now you're expecting him from the East."

"That's easily explained. He went with Captain Richardson to see Lee in Virginia and try to get the Rangers assigned to a place where there would be more fighting."

He relaxed. "There's been plenty of that—bloody, too."

"He was to be here the tenth of April."

"It's now the seventeenth," Talley said.

For an instant she looked haunted. "Do you suppose—"

Talley studied his cracked knuckles. "On a mission like that, he should get through all right."

She seemed to feel relieved. "When do you go back home, Mr. Talley?"

"Soon as I get my money—tomorrow, likely."

She brightened. "You'll be going through Marshall sometime—if you're not drawn into the war."

He nodded. "If I'm not."

"It has been pleasant to speak with you the last few days." She looked down at her hands in her lap. "One can be lonesome even in such a busy place." She looked up as a stagecoach stopped in front of the hotel, its brake screeching as the driver went through the customary flourish. "When you're in Marshall," she went on, "I hope you will stop to visit us."

"Maybe I will."

He saw two blacks go up the stairway with a wooden tub. "Mrs. Partridge," he asked casually, "what kind of passport do you travel under?"

"British, of course."

He got up. "A British passport will get you around Mexico very well these days."

She seemed puzzled.

"I'm going to clean up for the first time in weeks," he said. "Have you had supper?"

"Yes—but I would have a glass of wine with you. The days have been very long," she repeated.

He nodded, well-pleased, and crossed the lobby just ahead of the dozen passengers from the stage, and started to mount the stairs. Outgoing passengers to Baton Rouge and Natchez were moving outside, but he went on up, and did not know the fat man was near him until he heard a voice:

"Mr. Talley."

He stopped with one foot up and one foot down and turned around in the same motion. The fat man was half-way up the stairs, puffing a little. He came alongside and said, "You move so contaminated fast, Mr. Talley. Is that a characteristic of Texans?"

Talley scrutinized him. He wore an inconspicuous brown suit, rather warm for this time of year in New Orleans, and carried a limp white hat with a tall crown and a great floppy brim. Now he fanned himself for a moment, and Talley said: "We move the way we move, mister. Some people are almighty slow."

"Sure." He quit fanning himself. He had a considerable Southern accent that Talley could not place. "Mind if I walk down the hall with you?"

"Not at all."

They reached the top of the stairs, and Talley held back an instant. The fat man turned in front of him to the left, and Talley fell in.

"You're wondering," the fat man said conversationally, "who I am, how I know your name, and how I know where your room is."

"It entered my mind," said Talley.

"I'm a curious man," he said, "about some things."

21

"Are you curious about cattle or about me?"

The fat man glanced at him quickly. "You noticed me at the tally ground?"

"Yes."

"I'd like to talk to you, Mr. Talley."

"Come on into my room."

"Afraid I can't do that. You never know who's coming in on the stage, these days—and I might be seen *leaving* your room."

They were halfway down the long hall. "Is it important that you not be seen leaving my room?"

"It might be, Mr. Talley. It might be. Meet me in the barroom at Banks' Arcade, Magazine Street at Gravier, in fifteen minutes."

Talley frowned. "I haven't cleaned up yet."

"I know that, Mr. Talley, but I have some very important business to talk over with you, and I have to leave New Orleans in an hour and fifteen minutes." He pulled out a heavy gold watch and studied it absently. "Yes, I think Banks' is best. It has been a meeting place for conspirators for thirty years."

"I don't know about you, but somebody may wonder what *I* am doing there."

"Perhaps—but you will not run into them again." He said this quite calmly, and as Talley stared at him, he motioned with his thumb. "Here's your door. We can walk on to the end of the hall and back."

"You know a lot about me," said Talley.

The fat man looked at him, and for an instant a sort of veil seemed to lift from over his eyes, and Talley saw they were sharp and penetrating. "I hope you do not find it annoying, Mr. Talley."

"It is—unless I know why."

"Meet me at the Arcade as soon as you can get there—but don't hurry. I will go ahead. You go on into your room and give me time to clear the lobby."

They reached the end of the hall and started back. "I'll meet you," Talley said, "but if I get tangled up in any of the conspiracy and counter-conspiracy that New Orleans is filled with, I'll come looking for you. What's your name?"

The fat man seemed to stare clear through him. "Call me Jones."

"All right, Jones. I'll give you time to clear the lobby."

He went into his room. The tub was in the center of the floor, but there was no hot water. His cartridge belt was hanging on a post at the foot of the bed. He took the heavy Smith & Wesson out of the holster, turned the cylinder and made sure it was loaded, threw the pistol forward a couple of times with a limber wrist to weigh it thoughtfully, then decided against carrying it, and chucked it back into the holster.

He looked at himself in the wavy mirror. There were wiry patches of brown beard on his chin and

23

in front of his ears and on his upper lip; he was not the kind to grow a solid beard. He rubbed his chin, saw the dust sift out of his whiskers, and remembered the days on the trail when he could not afford the luxury of a good stretch. He went out and down the stairs, meeting the first of the incoming passengers—two gray-clad military men who looked very grave and weighted down with cares.

He stopped at the desk. "I'll be back for the hot water in a little while," he said.

The harassed clerk looked up from the register. "It will be ready, Mr. Talley."

He went across the big lobby. Jones was not in sight. He saw Helen Partridge, who had moved under a palm tree growing out of a wooden tub—probably to be farther from the door.

"I've got to go out for a few minutes," he told her, "but my invitation to eat still holds as soon as I get back."

"If you stay too long," she said with a smile, "I'll be hungry."

"Fine." He nodded and went out. He had been weary in his bones when he left the chute, but now, with several drinks of whisky in him, he felt loosened and relaxed. For a moment he wondered if this was Robertson's work—if Robertson was trying to get him somehow involved so the payment for the cows could be handled more advantageously to Robertson or to the Confederacy.

But Talley discarded that idea. Robertson was a Georgia gentleman who would no more stoop to a trick like that than he would cheat at cards—not even for the Confederacy. No, Jones had some scheme of his own.

He heard a woman arguing with the stagecoach driver. "Mah husband is wounded, and ah just have to get to Vicksburg to take care of him."

She was a young, black-haired Creole woman, very beautiful, and very much in earnest, but the driver was unimpressed.

"I'm sorry, ma'am. I can't take any but military passengers."

"But my husband may be dying!"

He shook his head. "I got my orders from the general in command of New Orleans. If you get a written order, ma'am—"

Talley walked past them, unpleasantly aware that the wife—she was hardly more than a girl—was weeping. Undoubtedly the war was moving closer, and it was a good thing he had delivered his cows. Now if he could only get his money before the dam broke. . . .

CHAPTER II

AT MAGAZINE AND GRAVIER he went into Banks' Arcade. In the long, dimly lit, well-decorated rooms, groups of men clustered at tables, engaged in low-voiced but intense discussion. A young red-haired man was leaning over a table talking heatedly and pounding with his fist, but at Talley's approach one of his listeners said a word that Talley did not hear, and the red-haired man ceased talking and sat up to glare at Talley as he passed.

Jones was having a brandy at a small table around the corner of the bar, from where he could watch all parts of the room. The man would have made a good Indian fighter, Talley thought.

"Glad you're here, Mr. Talley. Sit down. What'll you have?"

"I'll stick to bourbon."

Jones made a sign toward the bartender, and Talley sat down and pushed his hat back on his head. He was beginning to feel sleepy.

"What I have to say won't take long, Mr. Talley."

Talley yawned. "Enough for me to finish my drink, I hope."

Jones said quietly, "Having watched you drink, Mr. Talley, I feel sure it will."

"I don't know how you mean that, Jones."

"I mean it just the way I said it. For three evenings now I've watched you come in from the chutes, go to the barroom, swallow two drinks, and then go up to bed." He shrugged. "I have no criticism, Mr. Talley. A man drinks the way he drinks. The only thing important is that he should not make a fool of himself."

The bourbon came on a tray carried by a Negro. Jones tossed a silver dollar on the tray and waved away the change.

Talley toyed with the glass. "Mr. Jones, you've been studying me like a hawk about to strike a spring pullet. What have you found out?"

Jones leaned over. "Let's go back to Austin and Travis County, Mr. Talley," he said softly. "Your father bitterly opposed secession, didn't he?"

"Yes."

"And for that matter, so did you."

"I didn't favor it."

"It went a lot deeper than that. You fought a knock-down-and-drag-out fight on the street with Hugh Shelby, editor of the *Bugle,* because he printed an editorial about your brothers who didn't want to enlist."

"It was a personal matter."

"And they say you whipped him soundly."

Talley relaxed and drank the whisky. Jones poured another one from the bottle.

"The war is not very popular in Travis County," said Talley.

"Your father went to Mexico to avoid serving the Confederacy, but you stayed on the ranch to avoid coming under the sequestration act. Am I right?"

Talley pushed back the second drink. "I have complied with the law. I risked my life and my property to bring two herds of cattle to New Orleans so the Confederacy could have beef."

Jones looked at him, and Talley thought there was amusement in the man's eyes—deadly amusement. "I believe you told Robertson you did it for money."

Talley got to his feet, but Jones shook his head and pushed the full glass back toward him "You're acting like a buck deer in rutting time. I'm not trying to make you mad; I'm only trying to establish a common ground between us—to show you that we see things alike."

Talley slid slowly back into the chair. "Why don't you say your piece?"

"I'm getting to that," said Jones, unruffled. "But I wish you would consider me as a man with the same sympathies as yours."

"Talk," said Talley.

Jones took out his handkerchief and brushed the tip of his nose. "It is said around Austin that if it had not been for your ranch, you and the rest of your family would have followed your father. Now, don't answer. I'm not asking questions. You don't need to comment unless I make a serious mistake."

Talley said, "Maybe you made one by talking to me."

"I don't think so, Mr. Talley. You brought a double herd of cattle here for sale. At first I wondered why, but now I think I know: you wanted money so you would have something to take to Mexico when you go to join your father."

Talley said harshly, "You're talking like a damned Unionist!"

Jones's eyes bored into his, and Talley knew the man was making up his mind as to whether he could tell the entire truth.

"If you take your money for the cows, you will have something like forty thousand dollars when you leave Austin. But the Confederates will confiscate your ranch, which is worth several times that. Am I right?"

"I didn't say I was going to Mexico."

"Mr. Talley, we've got to trust each other."

"There's no reason for me to trust you," said Talley. "You may be a Confederate agent trying to get me to confess to anything so you can hold up the payment for the cows."

Jones seemed very pleased at this. "I'll lay my cards on the table," he said softly. "I'm a Union agent, and I have a suggestion that will make money for you."

"At whose expense?"

"The Confederacy's." Jones poured another drink. "Mr. Talley, let's say you will get forty thousand for your stuff, and let's say I can show you a way to multiply that by ten. What would you say?"

"I'd still like to know who's paying for it."

"Again I answer: the Confederacy. Let's put it

this way: the Confederate States are short of food, short of clothing, short of medicine, short of rifles and ammunition—but there is one thing whose lack will hurt them more than anything else." He leaned over his brandy. "Do you know what that one thing is, Mr. Talley?"

"No."

"Gold," said Jones. "Gold is the most precious commodity in the South—for with gold they can buy any or all of the supplies they need, and only with gold."

"Why not cotton?"

"The South is piling up thousands of bales in warehouses east of the Mississippi, but it has no value because there is no market for it."

"I thought the British—"

"The British would like to have it, but the need isn't imperative. They can still get cotton from Egypt and India, and they don't need Southern cotton bad enough to run the blockade and offend the Union—for there is no doubt abroad that the Union will win eventually."

"And since Confederate paper has little value, nothing can be bought abroad except with gold."

"That's right."

"And you are going to tell me—"

"How to turn your forty thousand into four hundred thousand, all in gold—and thereby strike a crippling blow at the South's economy."

Talley said slowly, "I don't know what you've

got up your sleeve, Jones, but I can promise you one thing: I have no intention of deliberately crippling the South."

Jones chuckled. "I'm glad to hear that, Mr. Talley. Now here is what you do: Take your pay in gold and take it back home and keep it where you can put your hands on it at a moment's notice—and not in Confederate paper. Is that understood?"

"Yes."

"In a short while you will receive a simple message by mail which will indicate that all is ready. You will then make arrangements with a Señor Andrés Díaz, a lawyer in San Antonio, to buy quinine."

"Quinine?"

"Yes. This fall it will be priceless—and every ounce must come from South America through Mexico City. When malaria strikes the South next fall, they must have quinine at any price—and I say conservatively that you should be able to demand and get at least ten times what you put into it."

Talley was silent, thinking about it.

"You will be under no legal obligation to the Confederacy, because you will be using your own money."

"It's a high profit."

"No higher than they are taking all over the South today. And besides, you will be running

31

plenty of risks. Mexican officials will stop you if they can. So will Union agents along the Rio Grande, and so will any one of a dozen outlaw gangs on either side. So you are justified in asking all you can get."

"How much does it sell for in Mexico City?"

"From eight to ten dollars an ounce—but you will have to pay more than that, because they will know what you are going to do with it. One ounce of quinine contains about seven thousand grains, and the pills are used in different strengths—from two grains to as high as fifteen grains. Say an average of ten grains—that would give you seven hundred pills out of an ounce. Now tell me, Mr. Talley: How much have you seen those pills sell for when the chills-and-fever stage comes on?"

"Last fall they brought two bits apiece in Austin."

"Exactly. This year they will bring a dollar apiece in Richmond and Memphis. And that adds up to seven hundred dollars an ounce, Mr. Talley."

Talley drew a deep breath. "It's good money— and it would be doing a service to the Confederacy."

"Are you interested in running quinine for the sake of the Confederacy?"

Talley looked straight into his eyes. "If I am—" He stopped, puzzled. Why was a Union agent

32

trying to arrange quinine smuggling for the Confederacy?

"If you go to the Confederate officers with what I am about to tell you, your trip to Texas will be delayed," said Jones.

"I understand."

"For the success of this smuggling," Jones said, "it is necessary to have the confidence of Confederate officials."

"I don't have that."

"You will be provided with a partner who does."

Talley poured another drink. "Who is he?"

"It's a she, Mr. Talley." Jones's voice was almost a whisper. "Helen Partridge."

"Hel—"

"No so loud, please. Helen Partridge is posing as a Confederate agent and has their confidence, but in reality she is working for us. She has money of her own—some twenty thousand, also in gold—to finance her part. Also, as you ascertained a short while ago, she has a British passport which will enable her—"

Talley's lips parted. "You heard me ask her that?"

"It's my job," said Jones.

"But her husband—"

Jones shrugged. "I don't know anything about her domestic affairs."

Talley sat back. "What am I to do?"

"Suggest to Mrs. Partridge that you go into partnership. She will do the rest. You will be watched closely by Confederate officials who will know that you have the gold, so I suggest you use Mrs. Partridge to make arrangements with Díaz. Then you will not have to come into the open until you start for Mexico—and you may depend on her to see that the Confederate officials are advised when you start for Mexico, so you will not have any trouble from them on your trip." He seemed amused. "We have the Confederacy on the horns of a dilemma. Gold is extremely scarce in the South—but they must have quinine, no matter what the cost. It is a situation that cannot fail to react to the benefit of the Union—and they are even forced to help us, by giving passage to a person like Mrs. Partridge, even though they know she will charge them beyond all reason."

"You said she is supposed to be a spy on both sides. How do you know—"

"We don't. The point is, Mr. Talley, she has this money in gold, and she is a woman who loves money. Besides you will be with her. You will be watching her—and you are a man of principle."

He went back to the hotel. Mrs. Partridge was still sitting under the palm. He said, "I'll be down in a little while," and wondered how she could be so calm. The hot water was ready, and he went upstairs. The blacks brought the water up in wooden buckets and poured it into the tub. He got into it steaming hot, and scrubbed himself thoroughly with a cake of brownish yellow soap and a rough cloth. The soapy smell was good in his nostrils, and the hot water soaked into his skin and relaxed him completely for the first time in six weeks.

Helen Partridge continued to sit under the palm for a few minutes. Then Jones came in, looked her way without seeming to notice her, brushed the tip of his nose with his handkerchief, and went on into the barroom.

She waited a moment more, then got up quietly and went out.

It was late afternoon of a warm April day, and there was much activity on St. Charles Street. Usually at this time of day the town had an appearance of sleepiness, with most sensible persons staying inside to avoid the heat, but at this moment the street seemed cluttered with horse-drawn vehicles: open buggies, a barouche and a two-wheeled cart, a six-mule stage coming in from the West, and an extraordinary number of open farm wagons. The clanging of iron tires and shod hoofs on cobblestones, the rattle of trace chains, the creak of leather tugs, the swearing of drivers—all contributed a confusion most unlike the usual atmosphere of New Orleans. No doubt the Federals were getting too close for comfort.

She went to Canal Street and the office of the general in charge of the city's defense. She asked the orderly if she could see the adjutant.

"That's Colonel Busby, ma'am." He scrutinized her with the eyes of a mountaineer. "Leave your reticule with me, and you can go in."

Colonel Busby was a kindly faced man with a gray goatee and a soft Virginia drawl. He seated her in a wicker chair and asked, "Now, ma'am, what can I do for you?"

She sat forward. "I was told in Richmond to find you."

"Your name?"

"Helen Partridge."

"Who told you to find me?"

"The Confederate secretary of war."

"John Randolph?"

"George Randolph. George *Blythe* Randolph," she said slowly.

He smiled. "Very well, ma'am." He took a sheet of pen-written paper from a desk drawer and read from it. "Height about five-feet-four. Weight about one hundred and thirty-five pounds. Black hair—yes, very beautiful hair, ma'am." He studied her and sighed. "I'm afraid, Miss Pa'tridge, the South has not taught its women to be anything but women and housewives."

Prudently she remained silent.

"Born in—"

"Kentucky."

"Your parents are now in England," he commented after glancing at the paper.

"My father fell heir to some property, and they moved back. He came from Sussex originally."

"But you stayed in America."

"Yes, I got work as a governess in Baltimore."

He put the sheet away. "I merely wanted to be sure you are Helen Partridge." He lowered his voice. "Your mission is to buy quinine in Mexico and smuggle it across the Rio Grande into Texas."

"Yes."

He tapped the report. "By the time summer is over," he observed, "quinine will bring a fabulous price in the South."

She was prepared for that. "It is not all clear profit. I put up my own money and I risk my own life. I have already smuggled gold through the blockade into New Orleans."

"Beggars can hardly be choosers," he said. "I am to help you—within certain limits."

"That is why I am here. I have a plan to triple my capital and do that much more service for the Confederacy."

"Yes."

"Mr. Randolph got full reports from the Confederate spy in Austin on a man named Tilley. If our information is correct, he probably will demand payment in gold for his cattle."

The colonel sighed. "If there is anything scarcer than quinine in the South, ma'am, it is gold."

"Nevertheless," she said firmly, "if he demands it, he is to be paid in gold."

"You have a scheme, Miss Pa'tridge?"

"Yes. He is to be paid in gold, Colonel—and he is to be thrown in jail on whatever charge you please. I will get credit for his release and he will be indebted to me. Then I will go to Austin with him, and by the time I am ready to go on to Mexico, I will persuade him to invest his money in quinine."

The colonel smiled. "The gold will do a double duty, and you, ma'am—you stand to make an enormous profit."

She held back an exhalation of impatience. "I repeat, Colonel, I risk my own money and I take my own chances."

"With Talley—"

"Talley is trying to be loyal to the Confederacy, but he does not have his heart in it. If anybody gets the quinine through the hordes of outlaws and spies along the Rio Grande, it will be I."

He shook his head slowly. "That might involve killing, Miss Pa'tridge—and you have the appearance of a gentlewoman."

She demanded, "How many thousands of General Johnston's men were killed at Shiloh?"

He sighed heavily. "That was war."

"This is war too," she said coldly. "That quinine

will save more lives than any general in the South."

He looked at her, and she recognized his distaste, but she arose and put a hand on his forearm. 'Be sure that Talley is paid in gold and that he is put in jail. I'll tell you when to release him."

She went out, took her reticule, unusually heavy with the derringer in it, and left. An old man like the colonel, she thought, had no business in a war. He didn't have the heart to kill a chicken.

Killing, she thought as she went back along St. Charles, was one of the principal activities of men. The war itself was proof of that. Then why not of women?

For a moment she remembered the light-haired young man she had married in Baltimore. As soon as he had put his property in her name, he had promptly dicd of "debilitating fever," induced by a series of regular doses of arsenic. The attending physician had been puzzled by the case but had not suspected the real cause of death.

While she was waiting in her lawyer's office for the estate money, she had read an item in a Richmond paper about the shortage of quinine, and it had set her wondering. A week later the war had broken out, and she had gone to Stanton, the Union secretary of war, with her plan. He had approved it and had given her safe passage through the blockade.

Stanton had approved for the Union because he wanted to drain gold away from the South. Randolph had approved for the Confederacy because the South would have to have quinine at any expense. Talley, she knew, had had something in mind when he asked her about the passport. Probably he was planning to use her in some way—but that was an arrangement that could kick in both directions.

She felt no qualms about her dealings. As a girl growing up in the red-light district of Memphis (which she never told), she had observed that money would buy anything. Money was made by men; therefore a woman was forced to use her wits to get it from them. In her mind it was only turnabout and fair play. Under such circumstances she saw no reason why all of the quinine should not be hers when she returned to Austin with it. She would hang onto Talley for protection until a day's journey from Austin, and then—she shrugged. Men were loathsome anyway.

CHAPTER III

TALLEY SHAVED and sprawled out on the bed for a moment, but, no longer burdened by the responsibility of two herds of longhorns, went to sleep almost instantly. He awoke to the sound of pounding on his door. At the first moment of consciousness he rolled onto his back in a single motion and reached for the six-shooter hanging in a holster from the bedpost. Then he remembered where he was, and sat up. "Who is it?" he called.

"Cap'n Robertson, suh, is looking for you-all down in the barroom."

He yawned—a pleasant motion—and said, "I'll be down in a minute."

"I'll tell him, suh."

He stretched, yawned again, and got up. He felt wonderful. Whatever the South was short on in the spring of 1862, it wasn't good bourbon. He put on his black wool pants, his knee-high boots, his buckskin jacket. He stopped to comb his hair in the wavy mirror. The wooden tub had been taken away and the floor cleaned up. He pulled on his hat and went downstairs.

The big lobby was well lighted by oil lamps. Four men, fashionably dressed in black broadcloth and fancy vests, played dominoes with the rapid skill of men who had been much on the road. A pompous man, with his feet on the fine table before him, smoked a cigar while he speculatively watched Helen Partridge, who sat in a corner quietly doing some embroidery work. She glanced up as Talley went across the thick rug. He met her eyes and went on to the barroom. He stopped for a moment, for the room was beginning to fill with tobacco smoke, and he saw that Claudio Dujet and his friends were still there. Then he saw Robertson, rather splendid in his carefully brushed gray uniform and wide-brimmed hat, and wearing a long, curved cavalry sword that nearly swept the floor as he touched glasses with Dujet.

Talley walked up slowly. The bartender leaned over the bar to speak to Robertson, and the officer turned with a wide smile. "Allow me to buy you a drink, sir."

Talley nodded and moved up to the bar.

"A toast to Robert E. Lee," said Robertson, "the greatest military man in the world."

Dujet's friends were quite drunk by now, and they responded with cheers and a couple of rebel yells and vigorous hoisting of glasses.

Robertson said genially, "Mr. Talley, your count was good. You had exactly 1,341 six-year-olds in those two herds."

Talley nodded. "I know."

Robertson slapped him on the back. Talk was rising around them like the sound of swarming bees. "You brought in 3,452 head all told. Is that correct, sir?"

Talley nodded. "I lost eight head in the Sabine River," he said thoughtfully.

"According to our terms, General Hébert agreed to give you top price for the six-year-olds."

"Fifteen dollars a head," Talley said.

"The way I add them up, Mr. Talley, it comes to a total of $42,265."

Talley nodded, frowning a little. He didn't like a spectacle to be made of so much money, for it was a long way back to Austin.

Robertson took a thick sheaf of paper money from an inside pocket. "Then we shall settle the transaction at once," he said, and began to count bills, laying them in a loose pile on the bar.

Talley made no move toward them. "Hold on a minute—Captain. General Hébert said the payment would be made in gold."

Robertson's lined face lost its geniality. "Do you mean, sir, that you will not accept Confederate currency?"

His voice was unnecessarily high, and suddenly there was quiet around them. Dujet stared at Talley, and somebody muttered, "Shaving the paper."

Talley answered fast. "I have every respect for the integrity of the Confederate government," he said, "but I deal with facts—and Confederate paper is discounted up to fifty per cent in Austin."

"We don't discount it here," Robertson said coldly.

Talley did not back down. "I have to buy my supplies from Mexico, and they demand gold."

Slowly Robertson put the thick package back in his pocket. He looked a little discouraged, and Talley saw that it had been a bluff. If a man had the nerve to demand gold, they were forced to pay it.

But Dujet demanded hotly, "Aren't you loyal to the Secession States, Mr. Talley?"

Talley swung on him, determined to keep the upper hand. "I am loyal, Mr. Dujet, but my mother and my brothers have to eat, and I have to try to stay in business and produce another herd of beef cattle by next spring."

"Brothers!" exclaimed a young man with heavy sideburns. "Why haven't your brothers gone to war?"

Talley turned to him but failed to stare him down. He was in a bad spot, for New Orleans had always been a nest of radicals and hotheads. He said to Robertson, "I can allow you time, sir."

"Time!" shouted the young man with sideburns. "He allows the Confederacy time!"

Talley, watchful for any motion that might mean a physical attack, looked at Robertson.

The captain's face was more deeply lined than ever, but he said sadly, "I'll have the gold for you tomorrow, Mr. Talley."

A little of the tautness went out of Talley. "I'll be at the hotel," he said, and turned to leave, but Dujet blocked him.

"I demand to know, sir, why a Confederate promise to pay is not honored in Texas."

Talley forced himself to stay cool. "I did not—"

He felt a rough hand on his arm, and turned to face the young man with sideburns, now backed by a solid rank of men, some of them in officers' uniforms.

Talley said coldly, "Take your hand off me!"

The young man laughed. He turned to his companions and said, "This is what they're sending us from Texas. What do you think—"

Talley hit him in the face—not once but three times. The man gave way, and Talley followed, slugging him hard with rights and lefts. The man went down, and then the entire room moved in on Talley. His eyes were covered with a film of blood and he could not make out faces. He saw a knife, and went in under it, knocking it into the air. Then something exploded at the back of his head, and he went limp. He knew they were hitting him, but it did not hurt, and he couldn't raise his arms against it. Beneath the mass of struggling bodies, he lost consciousness.

He opened his eyes as they carried him, feet first, through the street. Somebody said, "Get him to jail," and he stayed silent, for he was sure jail would be a safer place than anywhere else in New Orleans.

They took him through a hallway. An iron door screeched, and he was dropped like a sack of grain on a wooden floor. At that moment he would have given the entire $42,000 for his loaded revolver, but presently he cooled off enough to realize the absence of a pistol probably had saved his life.

He got up and tried his arms and legs in the dark. Nothing seemed broken, but his head was filled with a dull ache, and his face was bruised and swollen. There was dried blood on his left temple. He felt the back of his head and decided he had been hit with a whisky bottle, for there was a big knot on his scalp and the back of his buckskin jacket reeked of bourbon.

He watched the door for a while, but nobody came. He stared at the stars through a barred window high in the wall. Then finally he lay on the floor and went to sleep.

He awoke sore all over. He tried the door, but it was fastened with a huge padlock. There was no mirror and no water, so he sat down to wait.

The jailer was a thin, sad-eyed man with droopy mustaches. He shoved a pan of cold hominy under the door and said, "There's your breakfast."

Talley got to his feet. "What jail is this?"

"City," said the jailer.

"What's the charge?"

"Ain't none been filed."

"How can you hold me, then?"

"By keepin' the door locked," said the jailer, and went away.

Robertson came later, but stayed outside of the door. "I'm paying you for the cattle, Talley. Sign this receipt."

"I'll sign nothing," said Talley. "I haven't seen the money."

"I'll leave it with the jailer."

"Then get a receipt from him."

Robertson said, "You are not helping your cause, sir."

"When do I get out of here?"

"That depends on you."

Talley said coldly, "You mean I can get out of here if I agree to accept Confederate paper for my cattle?"

Robertson backed a step. "That will not solve it now. You have been charged with assaulting a Confederate officer."

"I wasn't the aggressor."

"It is a question of law."

"When will the trial be?"

"I am not sure."

"Not sure?" Talley swore. "Don't they still have courts in New Orleans?"

"They do, sir, but it is not a matter for the civil courts. Due to the threat of naval action from the Union fleet in the Gulf, the city is under military rule."

Talley controlled his anger. "Then you're just going to take my beef?"

"The agreement was to pay you in gold if you demanded. Do you still demand it?"

Talley advanced and took hold of the bars with both hands. "Where I come from," he said, "when they agree to pay in gold, they pay in gold. When they promise to pay with bullets, they pay with bullets and not with a whisky bottle at the back of the head."

Robertson flushed. "I asked if you still demanded gold?"

Talley shook the bars. "I sure as hell do," he said harshly.

"Then you will be paid in gold, Mr. Talley."

"Leave it with the hotel clerk, and see that it goes in the safe."

"Very well, Mr. Talley." Robertson stared at him. "When you get through with the military court, it will be waiting for you."

"*Military* court!" Talley pounded an iron bar with the side of his clenched hand. "You want to be *sure* I don't get my money!"

Robertson's face turned a dull red. "These orders are from higher up, Mr. Talley."

Talley watched him leave. If Robertson would put that money where he could reach it, he might escape from the jail and head for the Texas border. If there was a threat from down-river, affairs in the town might be confused, and—but Robertson had said the city was under military rule. That would only make it harder.

That gold would weigh a hundred and seventy-five pounds—a good load for a pack mule. There would be no chance to make a run for it. It looked as if they had him. He sat back on the floor and wondered when the next pan of hominy would come.

Presently he got up and began to examine his cell, inch by inch. He found that he could get out, but it would take time—and time was of the essence. That much gold was not going to stay in one place forever. He would have to fool the jailer into unlocking the door.

About that time two soldiers in butternut brown came into the hall and took up positions, one at each side of the door, with rifles on their shoulders.

Talley asked, "What am I accused of?"

The corporal said, "I don't know nothin' about that, mister. All I know is that Farragut is cannonading the forts down on the delta, and the colonel has ordered all prisoners guarded until they are transferred to Montgomery."

"To Montgomery!" Talley said. "When?"

"Tomorrow, probably."

"If Farragut takes the forts, how long will it be before he's in New Orleans?"

"Three or four days, they say."

"I demand to see the colonel," said Talley.

"He's busy throwing up defenses."

"Then I want a lawyer!"

"I'll tell the captain. That's all I can do."

The captain turned out to be Robertson.

"Did you deposit my money at the hotel?" Talley demanded.

"I certainly did."

"I demand to be released."

"The decision is not in my hands," said Robertson.

"Then I demand a lawyer."

"There are no lawyers available. Every able-bodied man is in the Confederate army."

"Except those," Talley said sarcastically, "who are hanging around the saloons picking fights with men who bring beef to the Confederacy."

"I'm very sorry," said Robertson. "The city is fighting for survival. We have no time to temporize with a man who is in trouble because he insisted on shaving the paper."

"Then you're taking me to Montgomery regardless?"

"Those are orders, mister."

Talley swore. He swore long and vehemently, but he was careful not to cast reflection on the Confederacy or on Robertson's ancestry. Robertson left, and the guards remained at their position outside his cell door. Talley sat down in a corner. He wondered a little about Helen Partridge—if her influence was strong enough to get him out—but he decided against sending word to her. It would attract Confederate attention.

That night he heard the sounds of a city preparing for siege—tramping feet, rumbling wagons, clattering iron tires on cobblestones, and all night long the hoarse shouts of men. He could not climb the wall high enough to see from the barred window, but the flicker of oil and resin torches cast yellow reflections on the window frame again and again.

By daybreak he faced the fact that only an unexpected act of providence would help him. His guards had changed at midnight, and there was no denying that they were alert. The guards changed again at 6 A.M., and the jailer brought another pan of hominy. "You better eat up," he advised. "The colonel is sendin' you across the river today."

"At what time?" Talley asked.

"I ain't snorin' on the colonel's pillow," the jailer said, "and so I don't rightly know. Anyhow, it don't make no never-mind to you. You got lots of time, mister."

Talley shook the rusty bars, but he didn't shout. Whatever possibility there was of escape depended on the guards' relaxing caution.

About noon the jailer was back. "A lady to see you," he said, and looked curiously at Talley.

"What lady?"

"I don't rightly know, but she's young and pretty and she brought an order from the colonel to turn you loose." He swung the door open. "See the sergeant in the office."

He went down the long, dark hall. A soldier in butternut brown was sitting at the desk. "Am I to be turned loose?" Talley demanded.

"That's my orders," said the sergeant. "Any complaint?"

"No." He hesitated, then repeated it. "No, not from me."

The sergeant motioned, and Talley stared as Helen Partridge came into the light.

"I heard you were in jail," she said matter-of-factly. "Haven't they let you wash?"

He felt the dried blood still on his face. "There's been water for drinking, and I drank it," he said.

"You'd better get your things."

"I had nothing but what was in my pockets."

"Will you walk back to the St. Charles with me?"

"Be glad to—if you don't mind the way I look."

"Not at all," she said.

Outside, it was like a city before a hurricane—men rushing in all directions, windows boarded up, wagonloads of goods headed for the Mississippi.

"The people are throwing food and goods of all kinds into the river," Helen Partridge said. "They say it's better than letting it fall into the hands of the Federals."

"They don't expect New Orleans to last long, then?"

"Not if Farragut runs the forts."

They turned the corner to the St. Charles, and he asked suddenly, "How did you know I hadn't gone home?"

"Because the clerk told me he was still holding your gold."

"My gold?"

"The money for your cattle."

"That hotel clerk hasn't learned to keep his mouth shut." He stared at her. "How did you get a release from the colonel?"

She shrugged. "I told him you weren't guilty."

He drew a deep breath. "There's one thing sure: if I want to get out of New Orleans with that money, I'd better start moving."

They went into the lobby. She stopped, with one hand on his arm. "I've checked on your horse. They've taken good care of it. I bought two mules for pack animals. All you have to do is wash your face, get your money, and meet me in front in half an hour."

"That isn't quite all," he said, watching her.

"No," she admitted. "It isn't."

He pushed his hat back on his head. "What do you want out of it?"

A man came in and rushed to the desk. She said quietly, "I have some money too—not as much as you, but all in gold."

"And you want to save it?"

"Wouldn't you? It's all I have."

"And you figure you can keep it if you get to Texas."

"From the talk I've heard, Texas is not as full of Confederate sentiment as some parts of the South—New Orleans, for instance."

"What will you do in Texas?"

"I'd like to go to Austin, I think, and open a millinery shop. It's the only thing I've had experience at."

"All right, ma'am, you got me out of jail, and I'm obliged to you for that. I'll see you get to Austin."

"I'm hoping that you will see fit to introduce me to some of the ladies in Austin."

"Why?"

She faced him squarely. "A strange woman at a time like this—I'll have to have somebody speak up for me."

"How do you know my word will carry any weight?"

"Next to Sam Houston," she said confidently, "I'll take a Talley."

He nodded then. "If we get to Austin, I'll see that you are introduced."

He went to the desk and got his key. He turned to watch her go outside and speak to the boy, who disappeared around the corner at a trot. She was a woman who could get things done; that was sure. He spoke to the clerk. "I'll want some hot water to wash my face—and I'll want my gold as soon as I come down."

"Yes, sir."

He washed, shaved his face as well as he could, put on his buckskin shirt, and buckled the gunbelt around his waist. He saw that the revolver was loaded, and went downstairs.

It wasn't until they were well out of town that he thought of another question. He turned in the saddle, standing on one stirrup. "What about your husband?"

"I heard yesterday. He was killed by Union raiders in Virginia."

He looked at her. A brand new widow but not even a tear. He turned back to the road. She was hard and heartless and capable—but she had a British passport, and that would be worth a lot when he tried to run quinine over the Rio Grande.

For he was going into it. He knew the lower border country as well as any man in Texas. He could find the paths through the *brasada* where most men would have sworn they didn't exist. He was the man to do it—but he would do it his own way. There was no question of his loyalty, no matter how the fat man had it figured. The quinine was a business venture—with a partner he would have to watch, for she was playing both sides of the fence. She was still a woman, though, and he saw no reason for worrying much about her.

CHAPTER IV

HE STUDIED her for a week. All day long she rode sidesaddle with a familiarity that could have come only from long horsemanship. They pushed the horses and pack mules thirty to forty miles a day, and Talley bought an extra saddle horse at the Sabine so each horse could trot without a burden one day out of every three. He noted with approval that Helen Partridge was easy on horses, and one night out of Houston, camped in a pecan grove, he said casually as he built a fire, "I've been told that you are interested in quinine."

She watched him. "You have been told correctly."

He went to his saddle under a tree and took the tin cup that hung from the saddle horn by a rawhide whang. "What do you know about it?"

"Not as much as I would like. I know there is very little in the South now. I know there have been heavy rains this year with lots of land under water. I know the medicine has to be smuggled in from Mexico—but I don't have any idea how that is done. I suppose it takes a man who knows the country and the people—and I have been told that you know both."

He worked the coffee can into the fire. "Mind if I ask you who told you?"

"Not in the least," she said. "Do you mind if I don't answer?"

He stared at her. "I was interested in who gave you the information about people in Austin."

"So are others," she said, and handed him her tin cup. This was one phase of life at which she apparently was helpless—the preparation of food—for she had not offered to do any of the work.

"If Farragut takes New Orleans," he said thoughtfully, "the Federals will probably control the Mississippi, but that won't make any difference to us. A pack mule can carry a fortune in quinine."

She said, "I'm curious about one thing."

He looked at her over his cup, held in both hands, with his elbows on his knees. "Name it."

"What do you want to get out of it?"

He studied his coffee. "Money."

"That isn't the whole answer," she said. "You already have money and you have a big ranch where you can make more. Why do you want to risk the money you have?"

He studied her. She was a sharp one. Well, it wouldn't hurt to tell her the truth. "I want to get my family back together," he said.

"Oh."

"Since I can remember," he said, "we've always been split up. Either my father has been off on an Indian raid, or with Somervell in Mexico, or in a Mexican prison, or on a pack trip to Guaymas, or fighting in the Mexican War. I remember how my mother used to sit at the loom at night, as long as the fireplace made enough light to see by, and cry silently because he was gone. My older sister was taken by the Comanches—and we never found her alive. My two younger brothers ran away to Africa on a steamship. Always there's been somebody gone."

"Including you?"

"Including me," he said fiercely. "There was no help for it. Somebody had to keep things together."

"But your mother was always home?"

"Mother stayed put. She used to say that some-body had to keep the home fires burning—and the way it looks to me, the others had all the fun and she did all the work. When my father got a little older, I thought that would take care of it. A man past fifty generally slows down. But the war came . . ." He paused. "My father lit out for Mexico; my brothers went up into the hills to hide from the enrollment officers. The whole family is all split up again."

"And you think if you made enough money you could get them back together?"

"It sure won't hurt."

"If I go in with you," she asked, "how will we divide?"

"According to how much each puts in. Say I put in forty thousand and you put in twenty thousand. A third of the net profit would be yours."

"When do you plan to go to Mexico?"

"As soon as I am sure about the quinine. It might be several weeks; it might be right away."

"I hear there is strong Union sentiment in Texas."

"Very strong," he said. "That is why Austin or San Antonio would make a good base of operations."

She looked up. "I should think that would make it more difficult."

"Not at all. With the country full of people who favor the Union, a man can smuggle goods across the border and everybody looks the other way because they figure he is making money at the expense of the Confederacy."

"Big war profits?"

He shrugged. "Who is to say what smuggled goods are worth? If Confederate officials think the price is too high, they are welcome to try it themselves."

She nodded.

"There is a risk," he reminded her.

"I imagine," she said calmly, "that with you in charge, the risk will be at a minimum."

He poured more coffee, and started to resume his cross-legged position, but his elbow hit his knee and half of the scalding coffee slopped out, and he straightened his leg abruptly just in time to avoid burning his foot. "For twenty-six years," he grumbled, "that right knee has stuck up a half an inch higher than I figured."

"There's plenty of coffee," she observed.

He moved to a different spot. "That isn't what bothers me. Sometimes it spills on my foot, and it burns like sin."

They reached Austin after dark. The town was three quarters of a mile from the Colorado River, and the main street was at right angles to the stream. He stopped the animals in front of Smith's Hotel, and went in with her.

"Why, howdy, Roy, howdy," said whiskered little Frank Ballard as he limped up from a chair next to the window. He shook hands vigorously. "We thought maybe the conscripters got you."

"Not yet," said Talley.

Ballard went around the desk. "They passed a conscription act, right enough"—he chuckled—"but everybody around Austin and San Antone is exempt, might' near. Some got jobs necessary to the welfare of the community, an awful lot of 'em got bum legs like mine—only mine come from a Comanche arrow. Anyway, everybody in this section is agin' conscription, and Reverend Garrison preached a powerful sermon on it Sunday. Got the Confederate recruiting officer some stirred up."

Talley put Mrs. Partridge's carpetbag at the end of the desk. "You heard anything about New Orleans?"

"Got word by telegraph. She surrendered the twenty-fifth of April. The Federals are running it now."

"We got out just in time. Frank, I want you to meet a friend of mine, Mrs. Partridge." He turned to her. "His name is Ballard, ma'am, and he'll fix you up." He told Ballard, "She got me out of jail ahead of the Federals and saved my money. Give her a good room."

"I'll shore do that," said Ballard, "though, to tell the truth, my rooms are all about alike."

He started off, carrying her carpetbag, but she turned to Talley. "What about my money?"

"You can turn over your money to Frank, and he'll put it in the safe. That's the best place until the bank opens in the morning." He hesitated and added, "Maybe better, because if you put gold in you'll get gold back. I'll bring in your saddlebags now," he said, "and keep an eye on them until you turn them over to Frank."

She seemed worried. "All that gold in the street now, unguarded—"

"For a few minutes it's all right. Nobody here in Austin would steal it. The outlaws in the country roundabout are the ones to watch out for."

He turned her horse and mule over to a black boy to take to the livery. Frank Ballard had followed him out, and now contemplated Talley's own gold-laden mule. "I'd be mighty careful," he said. "Things have stirred up considerable since you set out for New Orleans."

"Things have been stirred up since Texas first started arguing about secession."

"It's gettin' more serious. The Unionists are organizing around Austin and San Antone; the Secessionists are calling them names; and the Confederate generals keep askin' for troops to fight in Tennessee and Virginia." Ballard frowned. "The sides are too even. The whole country around here might bust out in a war of its own. There's talk of martial law again."

"I don't figure Texas ever did want to split away from the Union," Talley said thoughtfully.

"Parts didn't, maybe, but that's neither here nor there. There was an election and the Secessionists won it."

"Not by much of a majority."

"A majority is a majority, I always say. But that isn't even the worst."

"What's the worst?" asked Talley.

"Joe Cooper and his outlaws—and other gangs. There's killin' and robbin' going on around this part of the country, and everybody knows Cooper's gang is doing a lot of it, but the people are so busy fightin' each other that nobody goes after the outlaws." He squinted at Talley. "They say even Juan Medina was on the streets of San Antonio the other day—openly."

Talley gave a dry chuckle. "The brush country must be mighty peaceful with Medina out of it."

"No matter," said Ballard. "Mind what I tell you. Don't take any chances with your money."

"I won't. Now how about Mrs. Partridge's gold?"

"It ought to be all right here. I've got a big safe."

Talley took the saddlebags inside and watched Ballard put them in the safe. After the door was closed and the knob spun, Mrs. Partridge came down, and Talley glanced at his mule when they went out. There was no danger of the animal's straying—not after packing 175 pounds from New Orleans. "This man Giles at the oyster saloon has good food," he told Mrs. Partridge. "His crowd is a little noisy sometimes because of the billiard parlor attached, but you won't be bothered."

"I have heard strong language before," she said casually.

"Yes, ma'am, you probably have. Just thought I'd warn you. Wait up!" He stopped. "You wanted to be introduced in Austin," he said. "This is a good chance to start."

Three persons were approaching from the upper end of the street, and Talley said, "Reverend Garrison?"

"Roy Talley!" said a delighted feminine voice.

"How are you, my boy?" came the sonorous roll of a man accustomed to speaking in public.

They met in the dim light from the window of the hotel.

"We were worried about you," said Adele Garrison, "especially since New Orleans surrendered."

Talley touched the brim of his hat.

Then the almost lisping voice of Hugh Shelby, editor of the *Bugle,* came from behind them: "You must have pressed the *bayo* pretty hard to get out of town with your money before the Federals took over."

Talley looked at Shelby, a big man, heavy-framed, light-haired. He spoke with a slight sibilance, but his words always carried a sting; right now he was trying to find out if Talley had gotten paid for the cattle in gold. He was also at the same time implying that Talley had run before the Federal forces—as any sane man would have done. But Shelby was not a man to be concerned with right or wrong or good sense; he was a man to swing public opinion—preferably to his personal benefit.

Talley turned to Adele. She had the almost orange-red hair of her dead mother, and wore it in long, loose curls that lay nicely against the white skin of her neck. She wasn't tall; a girl like Adele didn't need to be.

"Adele," he said, "I want you to meet Mrs. Partridge, who is going to start a millinery shop here." He sensed Adele's coolness, and added quickly, "She got me out of jail in New Orleans."

"You're going to settle in Austin?" Adele asked quickly.

"I hope to." Mrs. Partridge's voice was husky against Adele's clear tones.

"It may be very difficult to get materials here in Austin," said Adele.

"I will face each problem as it comes," Mrs. Partridge said with assurance.

Mr. Garrison said briskly, "Well, we'd better be going along. We're having a meeting tonight to protest the conscription act."

Talley turned to Garrison. "From what I've seen of the Confederates recently, it won't do much good to protest."

"Nevertheless," Garrison said sonorously, "we are going to be heard. It is our God-given right, and I would be derelict in my duty to Texas if I failed to speak up."

"A Confederate officer and a staff of men are due here tomorrow," Adele said, "to enroll men from Travis County."

Talley said slowly, "An enrollment officer?"

"You *are* a loyal Confederate, aren't you?" asked Shelby.

"I am opposed to Texas' participation in the war, just as I have always been opposed," Talley said firmly.

"A pity you didn't speak out a little louder a year ago."

"My father spoke out."

"I hear your father's in Mexico where no enrollment officer can reach him." Shelby smiled insolently. "Your mule over there is loaded heavy, from the way it stays put. Did you bring back gold from New Orleans, and if you did, why aren't you putting it in the bank?"

"Where I put my money is my business," Talley said in a tightly controlled voice.

But Shelby would not stop. "Are you aiming to take the gold to Mexico?"

Talley lunged at him. He hit him twice in the face. Then Shelby backed out of range and his arm swung. His clenched fist landed square on Talley's temple and rocked him. He shook his head and swung in, furious, but Shelby caught him on the other side and knocked him at full length.

Talley roared up, but Garrison was between them. "Gentlemen!" he begged. "There are ladies present."

Talley, breathing harshly, brushed dirt from his sleeve. Then he looked at Garrison, small and stout, with a cane and a long, fashionable coat that came almost to his knees. He looked past him to Shelby's sardonic face with its heavy strip of chin whiskers from ear to ear. "This is the last time you'll do this," he said. "The next time you lay into me, you'd better have a pistol."

Shelby's head jerked back as he gave a snort of derision. "Talk wins no battles," he said.

Talley drew a deep breath and turned in a movement that included both Adele and Mrs. Partridge. "With your permission," he said, and wheeled on Shelby with both arms pumping. He caught the man off guard and drove him back. Shelby threw up his arms, then stumbled and fell.

Talley backed off as Shelby got to his feet. Shelby came up slowly. "The next time," he said, "I'll *have* a pistol."

For a moment Talley was tempted to hand his pistol to Garrison, but it was more important to get that gold put away—especially now that it was public knowledge. He turned back to Adele. "I hope I have not offended you, ma'am," he said.

She said hesitantly, "You and Mr. Shelby can settle your own differences," but her eyes were on Mrs. Partridge, and it was plain enough that Talley would have to answer for sponsoring the woman from New Orleans. He turned to Mrs. Partridge. "If you will excuse me, ma'am, I'll be getting on to the ranch. It's still a couple of hours' ride."

She said quietly, "I have imposed on you far too long, Mr. Talley. I will have no trouble finding a place to eat."

"I'll take you over to Giles'," said Shelby. "This way, Mrs. Partridge."

They moved off, and Talley said to Adele, "I'll see you in a few days."

She was watching Shelby and Mrs. Partridge, and asked in a low voice, "Why is she coming here to be a milliner, Roy?"

"Now, now," said Mr. Garrison. "Let us not—"

Talley held up one hand. "There's a great deal behind it," he said to Adele. "Don't make up your mind until you hear the whole story."

"We must be on our way," Garrison insisted.

But Adele turned to Talley. "Are you going to take that gold to the ranch tonight?"

"Where else?" he asked.

"That's a dangerous stretch at night."

He grinned. "Want to come along and side me?"

"That isn't so silly," she said. "I can shoot as straight as you."

"I'd enjoy your company, ma'am, but it won't be necessary."

"Please, my dear," said Garrison, taking her arm.

"Good night," said Talley. He went over to the hitching rack and mounted the *bayo*. He wheeled it and started up the road northwest along the river. The mule followed reluctantly when the lead rope jerked on its halter. He followed the little-used road up the Colorado River, thinking about Helen Partridge. From the moment she had told him her husband was killed, she had made no further reference to him, nor had she shown grief in any way.

CHAPTER V

IN AUSTIN, Adele and the Reverend Mr. Garrison walked past Giles' Oyster Saloon. Mrs. Partridge was seated, and Shelby was talking to Giles.

Adele said, "How did Roy meet her? She doesn't look like the women we know."

"Judge not," her father said unctuously, "lest ye be judged."

Adele looked at him. "I'll judge when I get good and ready," she said.

Shelby too was interested in Helen Partridge, but he noticed her coolness and did not linger, for he had other fish to fry and little enough time to fry them. Out on the board sidewalk, he heard Garrison clomping toward the hall, and ran after him. "Sorry, Reverend, I'll have to stop by the shop and pick up some proofs."

Garrison protested. "I thought you were coming."

"I'll be there before it's over."

"It won't be much of an argument if you aren't," said Garrison. "There isn't anybody else in Austin will speak out for the Confederates."

Shelby laughed in his throat. "Leave me room to speak last, Reverend."

"Father," Adele said severely, "it sounds to me as if you're more interested in the debate than in the principle."

"You do me an injustice, my dear—an ignoble injustice."

Shelby went into a side street around the corner from the hotel. He opened a door and walked into a dark room, struck a match, took the chimney off of a kerosene lamp on his roll top desk, lit it, and put the chimney back on. He turned the wick down to stop its smoking, and glanced at the still-damp galley proof his typesetter had left on the overloaded desk. The news was copied from the San Antonio *Express,* published two days before, but the typesetter had composed his own head.

"Capture of New Orleans. Farragut Guns the Forts. Jackson and St. Philip Silenced. Manassas and Louisiana Futile. Porter's Guns Too Much. No Hope Now of British Intervention. The Blockade Will Hold. Confederate Ships Too Light. Crescent City Under Military Rule."

Shelby rubbed his strip of bristly whiskers. There was something entirely too providential in the Partridge woman's getting out of New Orleans just before the Federals captured it. Strange too that she had come straight to the capital city of Texas.

But he had work to do—and little time. Partly because of the intense feeling over the war, and partly because of the shortage of candles and kerosene, Buass Hall would be jammed with people, some interested in the discussion, some looking for a fight, some just grateful for a place to go. With a packed house, it was all the more important for him to get back in time to take part.

He turned the lamp lower and left it on his desk so that any passers-by would assume he was around the shop. Then he went behind the drum cylinder press and out the back door. He cut across lots to Moore's Livery. Moore was off somewhere piking monte, likely, or maybe at the meeting, and that suited Shelby fine. He found his horse, saddled her in the dark, and rode out. He went straight west to avoid being seen. Presently he struck a road and turned north at a ground-eating lope.

Twenty minutes out, he heard a turkey gobble. He pulled up the mare and gobbled back. Then he let the horse walk a few steps, and waited.

"Who's here?" asked a low voice in the dark behind him.

He swung the horse. "Shelby."

"Get down. Stay quiet."

He followed a man into the brush. It was completely dark, especially under the trees, and he could barely make out the black shadow of the man before him against the stars. They followed a path through the brush and came to a small fire in a clearing. Three men were sitting around it. One had a rifle on his lap, and watched until Shelby came into the faint, flickering light. Shelby faced him—a heavily built man of large bones and powerful arms and legs; black, uncombed hair and a full black beard; a big head that nodded forward; dark, sharp eyes that showed much white at the bottom.

"What's on?" he asked Shelby.

Shelby said, "Get rid of the others."

Joe Cooper jerked his head. The three men got up slowly, with obvious resentment.

Shelby watched them leave. Then he sat down at the fire and poured himself a tin cup of coffee. "Roy Talley got back from New Orleans tonight."

Cooper worked off a piece of cut plug with his

strong teeth. He took his time putting the plug into his shirt pocket. Then he looked up, the glow of the fire throwing his dark eyes in deep shadow. "He sold the cows?"

Shelby tasted the bitter coffee. "Yes."

Cooper began to work the chew. In a moment he said, "Then he brought the money back."

"He brought it back, all right—and he didn't put it in the bank."

"He didn't bring it back in no Confederate paper, I take it."

"Not Talley," said Shelby. "I saw his pack mule."

Cooper looked up. "Loaded?"

"Loaded heavy," said Shelby.

Cooper thought it over.

"He's on the way home now," Shelby said in a low voice.

Cooper looked up. "Then we're wastin'—"

Shelby nodded. He finished the coffee and hung the cup on a twig stuck in the ground. Then he got up, a big man in dark clothes that blended with the deeper shadows of the brush. "He's alone," he said. "You won't need but one man with you."

"I'll take two," said Cooper. "One with me, and one behind him."

Talley turned northwest, keeping to the river. The hills were more broken up there, and the straight pecan trees began to give way to smaller and scrubbier cedars. He passed Schultz's place and

72

located the ford by a large cluster of cedars on the night skyline at his right where Schultz's road went over the breaks.

The water was knee-deep, and he let the animals drink, then went on through and rode along within a few feet of the river bank, as if at the bottom of a trough, for the breaks rose high on both sides. The mule was getting tired and beginning to pull back on the lead rope. It was a good thing they were nearly home.

The *bayo* was in a hurry to reach the barn, but Talley held it down to a walk and kept it on the grass, avoiding noise as much as possible. For a while there were few sounds but the soft plop of hooves and the regular creak of leather, against the incessant chirruping of crickets and the constant chorus of bullfrogs. Then it changed.

Riding along in the trough of the valley, he heard the sound of a dry twig snapping up ahead and to his left. He stared for an instant, then slammed his spurs into the *bayo*'s flanks and wheeled it in a tight circle. He felt the lead rope jerk against the saddle rigging as the tired mule threw up his head, but the mule, half pulled by the *bayo,* broke into a heavy gallop.

Talley stayed low over the saddle horn. They could not see him from the upper edge, and unless it was a well-laid ambush he had a good chance to go back a way, slip into the stream, and hide in a grove of willows.

He'd just got the *bayo* straightened out with the lead rope pulling taut in the saddle ring when a voice brought him up. "Stop in your tracks, Talley!"

This voice came from below him, and he knew he was silhouetted against the night sky. A man could not do very accurate shooting at night, but a horse or a mule was a big target. Talley pulled on the reins, leaning far back against the cantle.

"Stay where you are and don't move, Talley. All we want is to cut that lead rope."

He sat immovable, listening. It had been well-laid, all right. This man must have been waiting in an *arroyada* along the way, and had fallen in quietly behind him, riding an unshod horse in the grass alongside the road.

There was more crackling up at the edge, and he knew a mounted man was coming down—perhaps several of them. He turned his head to place the man below him, and the man said immediately: "I said *don't move,* Talley!" Two or three riders behind him at his right were crashing through the brush now.

Talley was still trying to make out the man. If he could get his eyes on him, he wouldn't mind gambling on drawing his .41. But he had to know where he was going to shoot. It angered him to realize that if either of the animals got hit he would still lose the gold.

He made out the silhouette of a man's hat above

the black blotch of willows along the river, then galloping hooves sounded a hundred yards beyond the man, from the direction in which Roy was facing. Two red-and-yellow splashes of fire winked at about the level of a horse's head, followed immediately by two thunderous reports, and then Adele's clear voice: "Keep 'em off, Roy. We're comin'!"

The man turned his head, and two more gunshots blazed in the night while the hooves pounded closer. The man's horse lunged forward, and Roy helped him with a shot from the .41; he heard the man grunt as the bullet hit him. Then Roy turned the *bayo* and fired over the mule's head in the direction of the men who had come over the edge. There were a few answering shots. The man who was hit shouted, "It's a posse! Run for it!"

Talley kept his animals where they were and waited for the "posse" to catch up with him. He said in a low voice, "I'll take over now," and fired his .41 a couple of times at the southwest sky. He heard Adele's "Whoa!" and got down from the *bayo* to hold her horse's bridle.

"Pretty late for you to be out," he said.

"It's just as late for you, Roy·Talley."

"But I know the road."

"And I know how the outlaws have been since you left. Anyway," she added, "I don't trust that Partridge woman."

He was amused, now that the tension was over. He stroked her horse's neck, calming it down. "So you rustled up a couple of pistols and acted as an armed escort, riding about a quarter of a mile behind."

"A good thing I did, too."

"I reckon there's no argument with that. Feel all right?"

"Fine."

"Then we better head for home. I don't think we'll have any more trouble with the outlaws. That was a pretty good act you put on. Fooled me even for a minute or two, until I remembered how you used to do the same thing when we were kids. Where did you get the pistols?"

"My father gave them to my mother when we came to Texas, to use in case of Indians. He always kept them loaded, so I just slipped on fresh caps."

He examined the mule. It was trembling, but probably from fright and fatigue, for it did not seem to be hurt. A final crashing sounded from the southwest as the outlaws broke out of the *arroyada* and went up over the edge. He heard their horses' hooves for a moment; then the night was peaceful.

He got in the saddle and started up the valley, keeping on the grass. "You can stay at our house tonight," he said, "but how about the Reverend?"

"I left him a note."

"Good enough."

He started up the bottom of the grade. There was a dull yellow light in one end of the dog-run cabin.

"Go on up toward the house," he said, "and wait for me."

She went on. He rode the *bayo* to the riverbank, and slid the heavy saddlebags off the mule and cached them in a catfish hole just under the bank. He went back to join Adele, and led her to the R Bar T corral behind the house.

He unsaddled the *bayo* and turned it loose. He unfastened the packsaddle and threw it on the fence. He took the rawhide hobbles from the mule's neck and sidelined it; he didn't think it was going anywhere, but it didn't do to trust a mule too far. He unsaddled Adele's horse, threw the saddle on the fence and hung the bridle on a post; he took the lariat from his own saddle and staked the horse. Then he tossed his blanket roll on his shoulder.

"Stay behind me," he told Adele. "There might be an ambush at the cabin."

He loosened the six-shooter in its holster and walked quietly up to the door.

He looked through the window. His mother had been sewing blocks for a quilt by candlelight, and had fallen asleep. She looked very small. He could not see her face, but her head, bent at an angle, showed her hair, parted in the middle and tied in a knot at the back. She seemed much grayer than when he had left—or was it just that he hadn't noticed before?

He looked down at the flat. He searched the skyline but saw nothing. He said in a low voice, "Come on."

He stopped at the door, called, "Ma," and waited.

Movement inside. The sound of steps on the dry, rough planks of whipsawed pine. The door opened and Mrs. Talley called, "That you, Roy?"

He stepped into the yellow candlelight. "It's me."

She watched him throw his blanket roll at the foot of the bed. "You got back—all right?"

"Sure."

He saw the relief in her eyes and knew she had worried. For a moment he held her upper arms and looked down at her. She was wrinkled and tired. A woman on the frontier was old at forty-five, and suddenly he realized that she was already old and that if she was going to have a chance to rest, it had better come soon.

He dropped his hands and said, "Ma, we've got company." He went to the door. Adele was still standing outside. "Come in," he said.

In the dim illumination from the candle behind the door she looked at him—blue eyes in a white face, clean sandy-colored hair—and stepped inside.

"Everybody in Travis County knows I got gold for the cows, and somebody tried to ambush me down in the valley, but Adele was riding guard a ways behind without me knowing it, and she scared them off with that old trick of playing like a posse."

Adele wavered on her feet, and Mrs. Talley helped her to a chair. "I'm all right," Adele protested. "I'm not scared. I'm just—"

"Relieved," Mrs. Talley said kindly. "I know how it is. I've been like to shake to pieces myself, after a fracas like that." She looked at Roy. "I dreamed the Indians were attacking. It must have been the shots I heard in my sleep."

Talley lifted the coffeepot on the stove and took down three thick cups from the shelf at one side. He filled them all and put them on the table, dropped a gnarled piece of mesquite root in the stove to keep the fire going, and turned back. Adele was still standing in the same spot. He made an abrupt gesture toward the cups and the table where his mother was already seated.

Adele's eyes turned to him. She walked forward to the table and sat down. She took one of the cups and sipped the coffee.

He watched her as she bent over, and he said abruptly, alarmed, "There's blood on your neck."

Adele's slim hand darted to her shoulder, and Mrs. Talley set down her coffee and got up. She pulled at the collar of Adele's dress and looked at her neck and shoulder. "You got a bullet across the shoulder," she said, "but it didn't stop."

Adele said nothing, but her lips were trembling.

Mrs. Talley turned to Roy. "Take your coffee and go fix up your bed in the other cabin. I'll put on some hot water and take care of her." He heard fussing as he went out.

The next morning he had to pull himself awake, for it had been a long and difficult trip, but he was up at sunrise. His mother was stirring pancake batter in an old crock, and Adele was down at the river with a wooden bucket. He followed her. "Feel all right this morning? Did Mother take care of the wound?"

Her blue eyes turned on him. "Yes, and I feel fine." She walked up the slope with a bucket of water.

He watched her go into the house. Then he walked carelessly along the bank of the river, trying to appear aimless, like a man inspecting his place after a long absence. Well out of sight of the cabin, he stopped to wash his face in the stream. While so doing, he tried the saddlebags and found they were still where he had left them.

The only danger would be from turtles or snakes, which might chew through the leather for the salt in it, but even then the gold pieces would merely sink into the mud. As unobtrusively as possible, and screened by the brush along the bank—for it was possible that Joe Cooper had a lookout up in the breaks—he piled rocks on top of the saddlebags. Then he slung the water from his arms and fingers and returned to the cabin.

Breakfast was ready, and they ate silently for a while, his mother getting up frequently to turn the pancakes or pour fresh batter. Then they began to talk about the ambush, and Roy noted with approval that Adele looked just as clean and fresh as she had the night before. He liked especially the warm, pleasant lights in her blue eyes as they raised to his.

After breakfast Adele offered to go out to look for eggs—obviously to give him and his mother a chance to talk alone. His mother shook down the ashes in the stove and asked, "Do you plan to leave the money in the bank?"

"No; if I did that, they would try to give me paper when I went to draw it out."

"What are you aiming to do with it?" she asked.

"First," he said, "I'm going to make a trip to Mexico for quinine."

"What's the object in that?"

"We own this ranch," he said. "It's a big ranch and a fine ranch, but we're going to need cash— and lots of it—to keep operating. We couldn't sell it now, for there isn't enough gold in Texas to buy it. But I can take this $40,000 to buy quinine, run it back across the border, and sell it for ten times what it costs. That's the best way I know to get it."

She shook her head. "Smuggling is dangerous, Roy. Feelings are strong, and the country is full of spies for both sides."

"That doesn't mean—"

"It does," she said patiently. "If they paid you gold in New Orleans, they've got somebody watching you now, and they won't let you take it to Mexico if they can help it. You know that. The South is desperate for gold."

He thought about Helen Partridge. "There are other ways," he said.

She fixed her eyes on his. "Roy, are you fixin' to meet your pa?"

"I might see him."

She said wearily, almost hopelessly, "I wish you wouldn't."

"Why?"

"Because I don't like running from responsibility."

"I wouldn't be running."

"He'll try to persuade you to stay when he finds out you've got the money—and it just isn't right, Roy. When you pick up and leave the country where you've done well and made money, just because you don't agree with the majority, then you're running."

"I never—"

"Your father ran away. He's always run away.

Why do you think we came here from Mississippi before the Texas revolution?"

"For opportunity—new land."

She said, in almost a whisper, "That was your father's story, but he didn't tell all of it."

"What's all of it?" he demanded.

"We had moved to Mississippi from Virginia. We got good land near Natchez and did well, but the governor didn't do things to suit your father, and we up and came to Texas."

He watched her.

"We did well here. Your father fought in the revolution and helped to form the republic, helped to join the Union as a state. All those things suited him—but secession didn't, and as soon as the majority voted to secede, your father jumped the traces again and went to Mexico." She paused, seeming to collect her thoughts. "How long will that last? Foreign people, strange religion, a gover'ment that changes every so many years. Where will he go from Mexico?"

"We don't have to live in a country where—"

"Wait. I want my say, Roy. You're only repeating what your father told you—and that's one of the things that got me confused. He talked too fast and he never gave anybody else a chance to think—but he's been gone a year now, and I've had time. I know what the answer is. In a country or a state, everybody doesn't go flying off in every direction just because they can't have their own way. That's why it's a democracy—because it's run by the will of the majority. You may not always like it, but you don't cut and run every time the vote goes against you. You stay and lend your strength, and maybe the next time the vote will be your way."

It made him uncomfortable. He'd never heard his mother talk like that. He got up slowly and buckled on his cartridge belt. "I'm going to saddle up the *bayo* and take a run up to see how the boys are making out."

She didn't move. He went to the door, and her voice stopped him there. "I want you to know this, Roy. If you go to Mexico to meet your father, I'm not going with you."

He stared at her. He didn't know what to say. "I'm staying here."

"They'll take the land away from you."

"I don't think so. It's still a country of law."

"What will you do? How can you run the ranch?"

"I've done it before. I can do it again."

"It'll be hard work."

"I've never known anything else," she reminded him.

"You haven't got any money."

"Don't you think my thirty years of being a wife on the frontier have earned me a right to a little of that money?"

He said slowly, "I always thought you were on pa's side."

84

"I was," she said firmly, "and I am now. But I'm not running away."

He went out slowly. He hadn't even considered the possibility that his mother would have such strong feelings about going to Mexico, but now he could see how it looked to her—that he was planning to move them all to Mexico so they could be together. Well, he had not planned it one way or another, but it looked as if his mother had made the decision for him. Then he'd get his father back to Texas. The family had been split up long enough.

CHAPTER VI

HE WENT to the corral and got a lariat. It was getting worn, he noticed; if they couldn't buy rope pretty soon, he'd have to make one out of rawhide, as his father had done twenty years before.

He went back down the river to the meadow where the *bayo* liked to graze. The horse was frisky, and evaded him for a little while, but he laid the rope across its neck and it quieted down. The mule, though it should have been tired, was more wary, as mules were inclined to be. It moved not fast but steadily around the meadow, keeping considerable distance between them. It didn't matter. He wouldn't need it until he was ready to go to Mexico.

He felt pretty good about his deal with Helen

Partridge. She had some connection with the Confederacy or she couldn't have gotten him out of jail, and he had no doubt that that connection plus her British passport would get him and his gold to the border and back again. Beyond the border, her Unionist connections were the most important.

He saddled Adele's horse and the *bayo* and led them to the cabin. The two women came out to meet him.

"I'm sure much obliged to you," he said to Adele, helping her up.

"You're welcome," she said, her eyes on his. "When that fellow pulled in behind you last night I knew the trip wasn't wasted."

"It certainly wasn't," he said warmly. "Come back to see us, won't you?"

She said good-bye and they watched her ride off. She waved from the bottom of the grade and Roy noticed that his mother looked sad.

"A long time ago," she said, "before you were born, I had a little girl. Her name was Comfort—Comfort Talley. She was a sweet little thing, but she got the chills—and we buried her in Mississippi just before we left." She seemed to look past him, at nothing. "My second was taken by the Comanches. I liked all my boys—you and Tom and Jim—but I wanted another girl." She shook her head sadly. "It wasn't meant to be that way, I guess. I was the only woman in a house of men." She took a plate out of the dishwater and dipped it in the rinse. "Adele reminds me of Comfort," she said.

He nodded and went out. He mounted the *bayo* and took the trail up through the cedars. On higher ground he was in the breaks—an area of water-eroded gullies, barren and desolate but for an occasional oasis around a spring. Back in the breaks were many caves, but he rode in the open as much as possible, holding the *bayo* down to a walk, not trying to be quiet. Presently, from behind, he heard a low voice: "Roy."

He took his time turning the horse. Standing in the middle of a clump of plum bushes, with only his head and shoulders showing, was his brother Tom. Roy moved the *bayo* back without hurry. Tom came forward through the thicket. He was taller than Roy, bareheaded now, and his buckskin jacket was dirty and ragged, turning black around the cuffs and at the elbows.

"How you coming?" Roy asked.

"We're all right."

Jim slid out from behind another bush and stood beside Tom. "You got back," he said. "What about the money?"

"I got it."

Jim dropped the butt of his rifle on the ground. He was a lot like Roy, but smaller and seeming to have little self-assurance. He was only sixteen. "Then we can git out of the country," he said.

"It won't be that easy," said Roy.

"Why not?"

Roy dismounted. "The Confederates are mighty particular about gold leaving the country. Besides, they're on the lookout for you and Jim both."

Tom exploded. "Hell! What's to stop us if we just light out?"

"Confederate soldiers, outlaws, and ten thousand Mexicans who would turn you in for a reward."

"I thought the Mexicans were agin' the Confederacy," said Jim.

"Officially, maybe—but Mexicans are like Texans. A lot of them look out for themselves."

Tom stood with his legs wide apart, his arms crossed over the muzzle of his rifle. "Are you tryin' to stop us?" he asked harshly.

Roy's look was level. "I'm just saying things have to be done with some thought."

"You've got a plan?"

"Yes."

"What is it?"

Roy asked, "You got coffee on the fire?"

"Sure. Up at the cave."

They walked up a dry wash and were on the cave before Roy knew it. A tall man, bareheaded, was standing behind a cedar with a rifle leveled at him. Roy raised his eyebrows, and the rifle came down. The man stepped out in the sunlight. He had a bald spot on top of his head. "We can't be too careful," he said. "The damned Secessionists are up to anything."

Roy went into the mouth of the cave. "I heard they burned your house," he said.

"They might as well," said Hamilton. "It's no good to me up here."

Roy sat cross-legged in the cool shade at the mouth of the cave. Sitting, they were hidden by a scraggly upshoot of bois d'arc and not visible to riders from below.

"What are you aiming to do?" he asked Hamilton.

"Since I was forced to come up here to escape the Confederate conscription, I might as well keep going. I'm heading for Mexico in the morning. Been trying to get your brothers to go along."

"We ain't going," Tom said, "until we know all of Roy's plans."

Roy looked him in the eye. "I'm not telling the plans."

"Don't you trust us?" Jim asked belligerently.

"What you don't know, you can't tell." Roy's voice was cool. He sipped the coffee; it was just right. "It's bad enough you knowing I got the money."

Tom's eyes were narrow. "You can do as you damn please, but I want my share now."

Roy shook his head. "There are no shares. It is

family money and it is going to stay family money. I'm not going to divide it up."

"Who do you think you are?" shouted Tom.

Roy poured more coffee. "I'm the one who has the money," he said calmly.

Tom was furious. His face was white. He tried to say something but couldn't.

Roy went on. "The minute we start divvying up the money, it will be a lot of little pieces. Right now it's in one piece and it's a big enough piece to be important."

Tom got control of his temper. "What do we do, then?"

"Stay right where you are and behave yourselves, if you're still set against the army."

Tom said sulkily, "If Pa was here he'd settle this right now."

"Pa isn't here," said Roy.

"Are you talkin' against him?" Tom demanded.

Jim put in, "Pa helped fight the revolution. He's one of the greatest men in the state of Texas."

"There's talk," said Hamilton, "of organizing companies of Unionists and going to Mexico in a body."

Roy was thoughtful. "I don't like that. A body of men would have to be armed, and McCulloch might take exception." He got up, looking at Jim. He wished the younger boy would listen, but there was no way to bring it about. Under Tom's wing, Jim would do what Tom said, and contrariness was part of Tom's nature.

"What if we decide to go?" asked Tom.

Roy shrugged. "Nothing I can do. It's your hide."

"Me," said Hamilton, "I'm going before they come looking for us."

Roy said, "I'd better not come up here again for a while. No telling who might be watching."

"Maybe Adele Garrison," said Tom.

Roy looked at him. "Meaning what?"

Tom smiled crookedly. "She was at the ranch this morning, wasn't she?"

Roy stood up straight, and his hat touched the roof of the cave. "Her privilege."

Tom got up, snorting. "Be damn sure you don't sell us out to some woman."

Roy, starting out, whirled. He slapped Tom with all his force on the side of the face, and waited, hard-jawed.

Tom's eyes blazed. He sucked air into his widened nostrils. His face turned red, with the mark of Roy's hand plainly white on his wind-tanned skin. "The next time you do that," Tom said finally, "I'll kill you. Brother or no brother"—his eyes were filled with hate—"I'll kill you."

"There better not be a next time," Roy said coolly. He looked at Hamilton. "So long, Jack. Be careful around San Antone."

CHAPTER VII

THE NEXT MORNING he harnessed up the team to the wagonload of corn.

"You better get some calico," his mother said, "while you're in town. Ten yards." She went on. "Sugar, salt, rice—do you think there'll be any coffee?"

"Maybe," he said, "but it'll be high. It has to be smuggled in across the river."

"I like my cup of coffee," his mother said, "but suit your own judgment."

He nodded. By sunup he was skinning the mules down the trace along the river. He reached the mill on the outskirts of Austin. The big water wheel was turning, for this was meal-grinding day, and there were a good many ahead of him. Old man Scott, the millmaster, showed him where to put his corn, and Eph Dunstan, one of the two town loafers, who never worked anywhere except on grinding day, got up into the wagon to help him shovel out the load.

Talley shouted at Scott, "What's the news from the war?"

The old man twisted his face and rubbed one hand through his beard. "It ain't goin' too good," he said.

Talley leaned on the shovel. He heard the water splashing over the wheel, and, from inside, the slow, steady bumping and grinding of the mill-stones. "How about conscription?"

"The Confederates sent men here to enforce it—a Captain Robertson and Lieutenant Dujet and a passel of sergeants and so on." He bit off a chew of tobacco. "Your brothers still up in the hills?"

"Yeah." Talley scraped the wagon bed clean and tossed the shovel to Scott. "Did you say Robertson and Dujet?"

"Yup. Know 'em?"

"Afraid so."

"Hm. They come here from N'Orleans. So did you. Well, don't look for anything rambunctious right away. They're startin' out pretty cautious-like. Prob'ly they got orders not to rile the countryside."

Talley drove on toward town, but stopped when he saw Adele Garrison taking an armload of wood into the kitchen. He threw a half hitch with the reins around a pecan tree and went to her door.

Her blue eyes were glowing. "Come in and have coffee." She said, her eyes going over his face, "It must be a lonesome drive, so early in the morning."

He pushed his hat back on his head and went in. "It's real quiet in the morning. Nobody up but the hawks and the bullsnakes—and nobody knows that better than you."

She poked a piece of fragrant red cedar into the stove and replaced the lid. "Father's downtown to see after the mail."

Her long curls looked nice against her white neck, and the blue ribbon on top of her head was just right. He looked down at her for a moment and then sat in the rawhide-bottom chair and watched her fold a cloth to put around the handle of the coffeepot. She was a little girl and well put together, he thought, as she reached up to the shelf for the sugar crock.

"Your shoulder all right?" he asked.

"Fine," she said. "It just broke the skin."

He held the cup with his fingers laced around it, drawing off some of the heat, cooling the coffee to drinking temperature. She poured herself a cup and sat down in front of the open oven.

"There's talk," she said, "about the money you brought back from New Orleans."

He looked up. "Nobody has any right to talk about my money."

She was a persistent little cuss when she wanted to be. "They say that so much gold could be used for the Confederacy's benefit."

He watched the wood glow brightly red in the grate. "What way?" he asked.

"They say that gold would buy quinine, which will be needed desperately by the South this fall."

He straightened so abruptly that a little of the coffee slopped out of the cup onto the wooden floor.

"Never mind," she said. "I'm going to scrub this afternoon anyway."

"Did you say 'quinine'?" he asked.

She looked up, blank for a moment. "Yes. They say it has to come from Mexico and can be bought only with gold—"

"I know." He cut her off sharply. "Where did you hear this?"

Her blue eyes were wide. "Everybody's saying it. There isn't a bit of quinine in the country."

He sipped the coffee. Adele made good coffee, even when she had to use half parched okra.

"Perhaps it isn't so much your money as it is the need for medicine," she went on.

His answer was abrupt, almost brutal. "Old man Scott is limping. Didn't he get that arrow head out of his hip?"

She faced him. "Roy, does it make you that mad?"

He said stubbornly, "I don't like to be pushed."

He finished his coffee. The front door opened and closed, and the Reverend Garrison, his round face red, bustled back to the kitchen and warmed his hands over the stove while Adele poured him some coffee.

"Conscription!" the Reverend muttered. "If they take all of our young men we won't have any protection against the Comanches."

"What's the talk?" asked Talley.

The Reverend hung his old silk hat on a peg. "They mean it, these new men. Adele, put three tablespoons of whisky in the cup. Coffee is so bitter these days." He said to Talley, "Anyway, have to have something to keep up my circulation. The mornings are still nippy."

Talley said dryly, "I've suffered from poor circulation myself."

"Maybe you—"

"No, thanks." Talley got up. "I've got business in town."

"There's a public meeting tonight at Buass Hall," said the Reverend. "You better be there."

"What can we gain?"

"If those who talk so much in private will talk out loud in meeting, we'll accomplish a lot. We'll show the Confederates that we mean what we say." He pulled a folded newspaper from under his arm. "Shelby!" He threw the paper to the floor. "Big editorial on loyalty and supporting constituted authority and all!"

Adele said, "I think Mr. Shelby is right."

"Right!" spluttered the Reverend. "Right about what?"

"He's for the Confederacy," she insisted.

The Reverend almost exploded. "He's for Shelby! He never says a blessed word that isn't calculated to be good for himself."

Talley said, "Hugh Shelby is a good man to play both sides."

The Reverend sipped his coffee bracer and muttered, "If you ask me, Shelby is responsible for a lot of the trouble in these parts."

Adele's blue eyes flashed. "He's trying to do

what's best. Texas voted for secession, and I think we ought to go by the vote."

Talley got up. "The principle is all right," he said, "but when it comes to Shelby—you ever saw a dog that's been killing chickens?"

Adele stared at him.

Talley said pleasantly, "Thanks for the coffee. See you at the meeting tonight, Reverend."

But Adele followed him out to the wagon. "Roy, what about that Mrs. Partridge?"

He loosened the reins and looked down at her. "What about her?"

"You brought her here, and you introduced her."

"I told you she rescued me from jail just ahead of the Federal navy."

"That's no reason for bringing her here."

"She had to go *somewhere*. Isn't she behaving herself?"

"Yes," she admitted, "but I don't like her. She looks so cold and so—so evil. And she hasn't opened any millinery shop yet."

He put one foot on the hub of the wheel. "If it's any comfort to you," he said, "I don't trust her either."

He stopped the team alongside a peeled cottonwood hitching pole in front of Hancock's store and went across the street to the Billiard Hall and Oyster Saloon and ordered a dozen oysters fried.

He ate his dinner in silence, paid for it, had a couple of drinks, and went into the hotel.

Two drummers sat in the lobby smoking cigars. One was fat and seemed unperturbed as ashes dropped down his vest. There was no sign of Helen Partridge.

Frank Ballard greeted him. "Somethin'?"

"Just want to sit down for a while."

"Plenty of chairs. Make yourself welcome."

Talley sat down.

"Live here?" asked the fat drummer.

"Yes."

"Things are pretty quiet around Austin."

Talley glanced at him. "It doesn't seem so, to hear the talk."

The fat man shook his head. "It's nothing to what it is in Virginia and Carolina."

"How does it look for the Confederacy?"

"Not good." A gob of ash dropped onto his vest and rolled down until it stopped in a wrinkle. "The South has no manufacturing. This year is going to see an awful shortage of goods—textiles, rifles, ammunition, any kind of iron goods, and medicine." He brushed ineffectually at his vest without looking. "The ague is already a problem."

"It sounds bad." Talley heard a light step and turned to see Helen Partridge.

The two drummers stared at her for a moment, then at Talley, and finally got up and went out.

She said to Talley, "I was expecting you."

"I came in as soon as I could—although it's too early yet."

She nodded. "I've rented a little shop for my millinery store."

"Where?" he asked.

"Down the street, two doors from the barber shop. It was empty, and they let me have it practically for nothing."

"Good. You're keeping your money where you can get at it?"

"Of course. I don't want to trade my gold for Confederate paper any more than you do."

"How are you getting along with the women in Austin?"

"Miss Garrison speaks to me when we meet, but otherwise they are leaving me severely alone."

He considered. That wasn't too good. It would be better for his project if Helen Partridge could be accepted like anybody else. He said, "There's a meeting at Buass Hall tonight. If you'll be there, I'll introduce you some more. They can't ignore you forever."

"I'll be grateful," she said. "I might be here a long time."

He watched her go up the stairway. Of course the women of Austin would have no use for a widow, well-dressed and handsome, who had come out of nowhere. But that would be remedied. He wanted the women of Austin to be a little involved with her so they could not so readily point a finger at anything she did.

He got up. Tonight should take care of that. The Talley name carried weight, and this was one time he would apply it.

CHAPTER VIII

DOWN THE STREET Hancock, the storekeeper, was standing in the doorway of his store. He rubbed his hands when Talley came up. "I thought you was going to pass me up," he said.

"No," said Talley. "I need some stuff."

"I hear you brung back something besides Confederate paper."

"That," Talley said dryly, "seems to be the most widespread news in Texas."

"I don't see much gold any more."

"How much discount for gold?"

"The prices are for gold," Hancock said firmly. "In paper it's more."

Remembering New Orleans, Talley said, "That's called shaving the paper."

"A man has to live. You can't stay in business if you sell at a loss."

Talley went inside. It was a brick building attached to the hotel. Groceries, salt, whisky, and bacon were sold on one side, dry goods on the other. At the back, under a rack of horse collars, a straggly-whiskered oldster had his bony hand in a cracker barrel. He looked up and said, "Howdy, Roy."

Talley nodded slightly. "Howdy, Jud."

A second man, fat and dirty-vested, turned from where he was cutting a wedge of cheese. He took a big bite out of the thin edge and said through a mouthful, "Howdy, Roy."

"Howdy, Eph." Talley said to Jud, "You got through early, down at the mill."

"He don't need me," said Jud, bringing out a handful of big crackers, "after he gits the mill to goin'."

The sweet vinegar smell of the pickle barrel was good to Talley's nostrils, but then it was overcome by spilled kerosene and the strong medicinal smell of horse tonic.

"Well," said Hancock expectantly, "what will you have?"

"How about coffee?"

"I've got it. Gittin' high, though."

"Ten pounds."

"I said it's high."

"How high?"

"Dollar a pound."

"Is that what everybody else pays?"

"A course it is."

"Ma likes her coffee," Talley said. "Ten pounds."

"All right." He got a scoop and began to shovel

the whole beans out of a hogshead into a tow sack.

"Ten pounds of sugar," said Talley.

"Still got your sweet tooth, eh?"

"And ten pounds of smoking tobacco."

Hancock frowned. "You don't need ten of tobacco."

"Why not?"

"Oh, I see." Hancock's eyes half-closed. "You got the brothers up in the breaks."

"Never mind. Just put that stuff up and stash it in my wagon. You got any calico?"

"A little."

"Ma said something with red in it."

"I've got it," said Hancock. "Made right in New England."

"New England? How'd it get down here?"

"Smuggled in from Havana."

"I wouldn't think—"

"Them big textile mills in Massachusetts and Connecticut would rather sell to the blockade runners for double than to the Union for one price."

"War," observed Talley, "is a strange business."

"Yes, sir. That it is."

"What's the bill?"

"Twenty-three dollars and sixty cents."

There was complete silence in the store when Talley thumped a twenty- and a ten-dollar gold piece on the counter. Hancock put the pieces in a long clasp coin purse with two compartments. "I'll have to give you change in paper," he said doubtfully.

Talley sensed the two loafers watching and listening, and said, "All right."

Hancock counted it out slowly. "You going to the meeting tonight?"

"Figuring on it. You get that stuff in the wagon."

"I'll do it right now."

Talley stopped him. "Where is this Confederate enrollment officer?"

Hancock looked askance. "Up over the bank, Roy."

At the same time, Captain Robertson of the quartermaster's department, very neat in his gray uniform but with vertical lines of both discouragement and determination deep on each side of his mouth, cut across the street to the hotel. A few horses were tied to the hitching irons—all plugs. He glanced into the lobby, saw it was empty, and then went back down the street, crossed over to the barber shop, went two doors farther, and hesitated outside the soon-to-be millinery shop. The door had a square pane of glass in the upper half, and across this had been placed a pleated white curtain. Robertson did not want to be noticed standing outside, but the curtain suggested privacy, and he was a little reluctant to open the door without invitation. He compromised by knocking.

Helen Partridge opened the door, looked at him, and said, "Come in, Captain. This is a public place. You needn't stand on ceremony."

He stepped inside. "It's a woman's place," he said. "It doesn't seem proper to barge in unannounced."

"Quite aware of the proprieties, aren't you, Captain? Will you sit down?"

He started to sit with his back to a small mirror, but she stopped him. "In here, please. It's not quite as public, but it's respectable." She pushed a heavy green curtain so the doorway was half open into her living quarters, and he went through. "Sit down, Captain. There's little business this time of day. In fact, there's little business."

He sat rather stiffly, not entirely at ease in the semiseclusion of this woman's quarters, even though he was entirely visible from the outer room. His wife had died early in the war, of malaria, and a widower led a lonely life at best. If he could be reasonably sure of Helen Partridge's loyalty. . . .

She had sat before a small table on which was a plaster cast resembling a woman's head and wearing a wig of black hair. She had arranged a wire frame on the head, and was now engaged in draping the frame with stiff black cloth from a narrow roll.

"I'm sorry I can't offer you more entertainment," she said.

"It is pleasant to be around you." He breathed deeply, "Nice perfume you have."

She was sitting where the light from a high window illuminated her face, half turned toward him, and she said, "That is kind of you, Captain—but you forget that I was once married."

He glanced aimlessly at his hands. "Perhaps." He looked up. "I like to look at you, but if I keep looking, I may feel impelled to touch you."

She looked around at him, but he could not tell what she was thinking. "You are honest," she said.

"I hope you will not take it amiss."

She turned back to her work. "Rather as a compliment." She got up. "I've got hot water in the kitchen. Would you like tea? There are biscuits and cookies."

"Cookies must be hard to make, with sugar so scarce."

"I don't use much sugar myself, so I have plenty."

She was back in a moment, pouring the water into the teapot, setting out a tray with two cups and small sweet breads and a tiny china sugar bowl. "Why do Georgians have such a sweet tooth?" she asked.

"Habit, I guess. But it really isn't necessary. I have learned to drink it without sugar on campaign."

"You would not remember me well if I gave you tea without sugar."

"I think I would."

"You may smoke if you wish."

"I have nothing but cigars."

"I enjoy the nice, homey smell of a good cigar," she said.

"Your—late husband—smoked cigars?"

There was an odd look in her eyes. "Yes, he smoked cigars."

He bit off the end of a Virginia stogie and lit it. He puffed a little. "Are you making any progress with your plans?" he asked.

"As much as can be expected. I am necessarily dependent on the other person, as you know."

"I have a letter from the quartermaster general expressing some concern, and hoping the first consignment will be delivered soon."

"You can't push such a thing as this."

"Isn't there *any* way to hurry it along?"

"Well"—she handed him a cup—"you know how it is on the border—and it is worse in Mexico City. They are saying openly down there that the South cannot win and that the Mexican government must preserve good relations with the Union."

"I've heard that," he said gloomily.

"So our biggest problem is with the Mexican officials. They don't want the Union to think they are allowing quinine or gunpowder to be smuggled via Mexico, for fear of retaliation."

He was a little astonished at the extent of her knowledge. "I will not ask you," he said, "for I have not been informed by the War Department and therefore I assume they do not consider it necessary for me to know—but I assume you are depending on this man Talley to handle the arrangements."

She did not answer, and again he wondered exactly how Talley fitted in. Had it been Talley's idea or her own? He felt reasonably sure, from the guarded communication from Colonel Busby, that Talley intended to use his own gold for the quinine venture, and he thought Talley probably had more money to risk than Mrs. Partridge, but there were still many details he did not understand. "If so," he said, "I hope you will not trust him any more than you have to. Three of the family are Union sympathizers."

"I never trust anybody more than I have to," she said coldly.

He laid his cigar across the edge of the saucer at his elbow. "Can you give me any encouragement that you might get started soon?"

She took a bite of biscuit. "Captain, one must develop patience in any sort of enterprise. When the quinine is ready, Talley will be notified. Until then we can only wait."

She had told him little, and she intended to tell him little. Meanwhile, he had learned at least that Talley was in on it. He finished his tea, picked up his cigar, and took his hat from the floor.

"So soon?" she asked.

He nodded slowly, watching her.

"You'll be back tomorrow?"

"If I may," he said.

He left feeling encouraged. He wanted to trust Mrs. Partridge, in spite of Colonel Busby's instructions, and he didn't like this snooping into her affairs.

He went back across the street to the bank. He went up the outside stairway, opened the door at the top, and stepped into a dim hallway. He pushed open a door and went in. Lieutenant Dujet looked up. "A man to see you, sir—a man you may remember."

There was something unusual, almost vengeful, in Dujet's voice. He went around his desk, sat down in the big chair, and said to the man waiting: "Want to see me, sir?"

"I heard talk about me and my brothers. I came to find out what there is to it."

The voice was familiar. The man was of medium height, inclined to smallishness but well put together. He wore shapeless dark woolen pants, a deerskin shirt, and a neat dun-colored hat, not very wide of brim but rather tall of crown and seeming to fit very tightly on his head. "You're—"

"Roy Talley."

"Talley? Sure." He got up to shake hands. "I bought some beef from you."

"That's what you did—3,452 head all told."

"You have quite a memory for figures, Mr. Talley."

"About cows, yes. Cows are my business."

"Have a cigar?"

Talley didn't move anything but his lips. "No, thanks."

"Well," said Robertson, "I imagine everybody knows why I'm in Austin."

"The country is full of spies," Talley said without emotion. "Every move anybody makes is reported."

"I'm not a spy," Robertson said firmly. "I'm here to get more troops for the Confederate army, and I'm hoping to do it without arousing hard feelings."

"You can't take men away from their families without that!"

Robertson shrugged. "I make no pretense that it will be pleasant. War is a nasty business—but we are all in this together and we've all got to pull our part of the load."

"Maybe some don't believe it's right."

"Well," said Robertson, "the Confederacy has made regulations under which those who do not want to live in the Confederacy may go to the Union."

"Yes," said Talley. "You give them forty days to get out, and you confiscate their property."

"What do you expect in a time of war—to be handled with kid gloves?"

"They have no right to take property."

Robertson murmured, "You have forty thousand acres up on the river. Your land is in the Confederacy, isn't it? You made your money here, didn't you? Then by what right can you turn against the country?"

"I'm not saying I'm against it, myself, but some maintain they have a right to think as free men."

"They have that right," Robertson conceded, "but not the right to take goods or property or money to the enemy in time of war. Frankly, I do not think that any established rules of war require us to allow enemy sympathisers to leave the country at all. And as a matter of fact, I do not think that practice will long continue."

"You mean people will be *forced* to stay in Texas?"

"Is that so bad? You were born in Texas. Your father came here of his own free will and built up one of the most valuable estates in the country."

Talley took a deep breath. Finally he said, "What if the people of Texas refuse to contribute troops, Captain?"

Robertson sensed the hotheadedness of Dujet at his back, but he remained calm. He carefully turned his cigar against the edge of a tray until the ash came off. "Then the War Department will have no choice but to send troops into Texas to enforce conscription." He was on thin ice there and he knew it. The War Department needed every man it could get in Tennessee and Virginia, and his job was to get enlistments in Travis County without trouble. But theoretically the answer was correct.

"Texas fought one war," Talley reminded him, "and whipped Mexico."

Robertson said softly, "We are not Mexicans fighting for a would-be emperor, Mr. Talley; we are the same kind of men as you, and we are fighting for our liberty."

Talley continued to stare at him for a moment, and then asked in that same level voice, "What do you want from me?"

Robertson glanced at a paper on his desk. "There are four adult males in your family, all supposedly in good health."

"My father went to Mexico."

"That still leaves three. I'm afraid we cannot eliminate your brothers just because they are hiding up in the breaks."

"We are running a ranch. Where do you think those thirty-four hundred head of cows came from, and how do you think we are going to work the cattle this fall and next spring? Won't the Confederacy be wanting more beef?"

"It seems out of place to me," Robertson observed, "that from three men you cannot furnish one soldier. You can hire older men or boys to work on the ranch."

"And pay them with what?"

"You have forty thousand dollars in gold," Robertson pointed out, "which you have not put in the bank for fear of having to exchange it for paper money. You could hire a lot of help with that."

He saw Talley's lips tighten. He knew fairly well, of course, that Talley was going to use that money for quinine, but he did not dare reveal that. "You are not the only family that has men hiding in the hills. There's A. J. Hamilton, for one."

Talley said stubbornly, "There'll be trouble around Austin if you try to conscript them by force."

"The Confederacy can't wait forever. There will be campaigns this winter. The Army of the Cumberland will make a determined attack on Vicksburg—and we cannot hold them off without men." He took the cigar out of his mouth. "I was at Shiloh, Mr. Talley, where the Confederacy lost ten thousand fighting men—most of them dead. We also lost a great victory which might have been ours with just a little more strength. If we had had a couple of more brigades to reinforce Hardee and Bragg, we might have beaten Sherman and Grant and turned the entire tide of war. It was a bloody battle, Mr. Talley. I saw entire trees stripped of their leaves by rifle fire; I saw gullies running with blood, men dead and men dying; I carried away three rifle balls myself—and I still carry them." He went on softly, "I saw five men out of one family killed at Shiloh, Mr. Talley—piled up, one on another. Would you blame me if I got impatient?"

But Talley was not ready to give up. "There are men like Shelby—"

"He's editing a newspaper," Robertson eyed him patiently. "Mr. Talley, there are *three* able men in your family. I hope to hear from one of you soon."

Talley got up slowly. Robertson thought he looked a little discouraged; perhaps he had made an impression after all.

"One thing I'd like to ask, Captain," said Talley.

"All right."

"Do you know Captain Richardson of Lane's Rangers, who went to Virginia this year to see Lee?"

"I know about it."

"Did Richardson have anybody with him?"

"An aide."

"Do you remember his name?"

Robertson said slowly, "Fletcher, I think. Sergeant Fletcher."

"And nobody else?"

"Nobody else."

"Not a man named Partridge?"

"Partridge?" For an instant Richardson stared at him. "No. Richardson made two trips, and his aide both times was Sergeant Fletcher. Why?"

"Curious," said Talley. "Just curious." He turned to leave.

"I hope to hear from you soon," said Robertson again.

Talley got up. "You may hear from me," he said and went out.

"Hardheaded customer," observed Robertson.

Dujet sprang to his feet. "Let me go after him, Captain. I'll—"

"You'll what?" asked Robertson, staring at the lieutenant. "I should think you had enough of Roy Talley in New Orleans. He was whipping four of you until Romaine broke the whisky bottle over his head."

Dujet subsided, and Robertson felt sorry for him. "Anyway, I have other plans for Talley," he said.

"Then why do you throw it into him about enlisting?"

"Because I don't want him to know what I'm thinking."

"You're a deep one, Captain."

Robertson regarded him calmly. "I've got a job to do, and I hope to do it the way that works best."

Outside, Talley went slowly toward the post office. It began to look as if the Confederates meant business. His eyes narrowed as he recalled Robertson's mention of the gold. The captain had that foremost in his mind, and Talley wondered if

Robertson would try to set a trap for him when he started for Mexico. Just how much weight could Helen Partridge be expected to have with him? Not much, likely. Her real value was in the possession of that British passport. They might never be challenged in Mexico, but if they were, the passport would be indispensable.

CHAPTER IX

THERE WAS a small group of men in the post office, and the windows were down. "Mail come on horseback from Houston," said Eph Dunstan. "They're putting it up now."

Talley listened to the talk.

"—organizing Unionist leagues all over the state," said the fat drummer.

"To fight the Confederates?"

"To keep from being conscripted. Who wants to fight his kin on the other side?"

Paul Scarbrough, a tall, well-dressed young lawyer who had read law in New York and had come down a few years before, said to them all, "I don't like being forced to fight against my convictions, but I think we should support the government that protects us."

"*You* ain't gone yet," said Frank Ballard.

"I told Robertson I was ready to go when he wanted me."

"You," said Eph, "are a traitor to Texas."

Scarbrough looked at him. "If you were not an old man," he said, "I'd take you apart for saying that. But you *are* an old man, so I'll just say you're a rabble rouser. You'll fight on any side as long as you don't get hurt."

"I ain't goin' to take that off of you!"

"Then don't hand it out."

Talley stepped forward. "He's right, Eph. You don't fight for principle. You don't fight at all. You're good at sicking somebody else on, but you never get hurt yourself and you know it."

That stopped them for a while. They broke into small groups and began to talk about the Unionist Leagues. Up in Fayette County they had formed a home guard unit, the Silver Grays, and were drilling two days a week. All members of the Silver Grays expected to be exempt from military service in the theater of war, on the theory that they were protecting Texas from the Indians and Mexicans. The idea had spread. There were Iron Grays, Dapple Grays, and Gray Guards. But some predicted the Confederacy would not accept the evasion.

There was dissatisfaction with the conscription law in general, though it had not been enforced yet in Texas. "If you've got money," said B. B. Davis, a lanky one-gallused farmer, "you can buy a substitute. But who's got that much money in Texas?"

"Gentlemen," said the drummer, "you don't

116

know what war is until you've been in some of the states where they're fighting. This here's a picnic, compared. There's no bandages, so they tear up the sheets and sleep on the bare ground—and in Mississippi a month ago I saw people eating bread in the dark so they wouldn't see the weevils."

They stared at him.

"It's a fact," said the thin drummer. "Women going to church in dresses made out of tow sacks. Men wearing bloody bandages all over town. I tell you, they been hit hard."

The general delivery window slammed up, and the postmaster, in black sateen sleeves and green eyeshade, called, "Who's first?"

"I been here the longest," said B. B. Davis, bending down to look in the window.

The postmaster ran through a small handful of mail.

"Nothing for you. Next."

"Confederates can't even bring a man any mail," Davis grumbled.

"Talley?" asked the postmaster, looking up. "Here's one for you."

Talley turned it over in his hands. A green Confederate stamp was on the envelope, which was addressed in a very fancy handwriting. He went to one side, tore off the end, and took out a folded sheet of paper. It was dated "San Antonio de Béxar," and said: *Muy señor mío:* Attorneys

117

for the Monterrey Land and Cattle Company have expressed their desire to make a settlement with you. I advise you give this your attention as soon as possible. *Su seguro servidor,* Andrés Díaz, Lawyer."

He put the letter back in the envelope, folded it double, and put it inside of his shirt. He drove out to the mill and got his cornmeal, then back to the hotel for supper. Dr. Kenedy was eating in there, and Talley sat down across from him.

"Busy these days, doc?"

"Tol'able," said Kenedy. "Nothin' ever seems to stop babies."

"Look for ague this fall?"

"Not as much as farther east. It hasn't been too wet around here—but we'll have some, never fear."

"How about quinine?"

"Don't know where it's comin' from."

Kenedy finished his meal and left. Talley ate, watched a pool game, and walked down to the hall after dark.

The platform was pretty well lighted with oil lamps, and there were a few men sitting in the hall, though it was early. Among them were the two drummers and B. B. Davis. Talley took a seat near the back.

The Reverend Garrison came in, his round, shining face flushed as usual. Adele was on his arm, very pretty in a small, light blue hat, and she went up to the platform with him. Shelby entered a few minutes later and ambled up carelessly, sitting on the opposite side. Those two, then, were to debate.

There was a flurry at the door, and Helen Partridge came in. She stood there and looked around until she caught Talley's eyes. He got up and went to meet her.

"You said I should come," she said evenly.

"Sure." He looked around. He might as well start big. He didn't see Mrs. Lubbock, the governor's wife, and figured she would not be there as a matter of policy, but he saw somebody else, and guided Mrs. Partridge over to her. "Mrs. Clark," he said, "I want you to meet Mrs. Partridge, the new milliner in Austin."

He saw Mrs. Clark hesitate, but he had counted on the weight of the Talley name, and it worked. Mrs. Clark said she was glad to meet Mrs. Partridge, and could she stop in some day and look at her hats, and Mrs. Partridge asked her in for tea.

"Mrs. Clark," he said finally, "is the wife of the governor who filled out Sam Houston's term when Houston would not take the oath of allegiance to the Confederacy."

Helen Partridge said, "I heard about that. Texas owes your husband a debt of gratitude, Mrs. Clark."

Mrs. Clark felt better, and Roy looked up to the

platform. Adele was watching them, tight-lipped. Talley motioned to her. She got up slowly and came to meet him.

"Will you take Mrs. Partridge around and introduce her?" he asked.

She said, "Roy, I don't understand you at all."

"Make it a favor to me—please."

Adele's lips were tight. "Roy Talley, some day you'll ask me to do too much." But she went up to Mrs. Partridge and took charge of her.

The hall was well-filled, and Adele took her around to Paul and Mrs. Scarbrough, Mrs. Hamilton, Mrs. Hancock, the postmaster's wife, and everybody else she could see. Then Adele went back to the platform, and Talley made room for Mrs. Partridge beside him. Adele's face looked whiter than usual, but he asked Helen Partridge, "Satisfied?"

"You couldn't have done better," she said.

"Then we're even now for you getting me out of jail?"

"Oh, you never owed me anything for that."

He glanced at her. "There might be more truth than poetry in that," he said.

She was instantly alert. "What do you mean?"

He sidetracked it. "Maybe they were ready to turn me loose anyway."

Scarbrough got up on the platform. The hall was crowded. The front row was filled with children, and there were adults standing along the back wall—among them Ned Hungerford and Jesús, both of whom were known to be members of Joe Cooper's gang. Even with the traditional animosity between Texan and Mexican, a Sonora-born man like Jesús was acceptable among a gang of outlaws, Roy noted.

They were there, Paul Scarbrough said, to debate the question: "Resolved: That Texas should secede from the Confederacy." He emphasized that the meeting should aim at understanding and a meeting of minds—not conflict. Then he introduced the Reverend Garrison.

Garrison's bald pate was shiny in the yellow light. He went up to the speakers' table, cleared his throat, arranged his various sheets of paper, cleared his throat again, and commenced:

"Ladies and gentlemen, I am here tonight not to debate a political question, but to speak on the far more important question of whether a man is the master of his own soul." He cleared his throat and looked around. B. B. Davis rolled out a vigorous "Amen!" and the crowd settled back for the fireworks.

"It is not a question," Garrison said, glaring like an actor, "of secession from the Union *or* from the Confederacy. It is a question of controlling our own destiny. I hold that if the South had the right to secede from the Union, then Texas has a right to secede from the South." He slammed the table with his fist. "I agree with Sam Houston that we should set up the Republic of Texas the way it was twenty-five years ago." He paused for a drink of water. "Are we going to have men coming into this sovereign state from Georgia and Virginia and Tennessee and tell us how to run our affairs?" He hammered the table with his fist. "At this moment," he shouted, "a Creole Frenchman from Louisiana, General Hébert, is in command of our lives, our rights, and our freedom. Is this the undying privilege for which we whipped England back in '76?"

A roar of approval went up.

"I demand to know," Garrison bellowed, "if Texans are going to submit to foreigners, allow them to conscript us into the army and send us to fight and die on foreign battlefields, to tell us what kind of money we have to use, or insult our wives and daughters, with absolute immunity from the law."

The hall was in an uproar for several minutes. Talley looked around for Robertson but did not see him. Robertson must have known this crowd would be inflamed.

Presently Shelby got up, slouchy, clothes wrinkled, his hair falling over his ears, his thick fringe of whiskers untrimmed, and began to speak in his peculiar sibilant voice:

"I cannot call the Reverend a liar," he began, "for he is a preacher, and as everybody knows, a preacher does not lie." A shocked silence. "But I call to his mind that Texas did not vote to fight a war; she merely voted to secede along with the others. South Carolina did not vote to go to war; she was forced to fight to defend herself. I call on every honest and fair-minded man to bear witness to the fact that the Union deliberately and intentionally provoked an attack by sending troops and supplies into position to menace the South."

There was still silence.

"When one state was attacked, what else was there for the South to do but fight back? Is each state to wait its turn and let the capitalists from the North swallow us up one at a time?" He paused. "Our only hope," he thundered, "is to band together as Americans have always banded together, and fight back as a unit, side by side. Our only hope is to support each other. With men like the dictator General Frémont and the bloodthirsty General McClellan, who calls for hundreds of thousands of soldiers to crush our boys in gray, or the inhuman Grant with his barrels of whisky—with these hordes attacking us from the north and west, what possible chance has any state to stand alone? We would fall like ninepins."

Another moment of silence, and Talley knew that a few were thinking about what Shelby had said, but most of them were trying to think up an answer. Finally Mumpy Moore shouted, "How about the conscription? Are we going to let these dirty rats come in here and take our men away to die in Tennessee?"

"Conscription is necessary when you fight a war. It applies to every state in the Confederacy—not just Texas. What is fair for one is fair for all."

"*You* ain't fightin' under Longstreet," said a farmer named Abraham Tilden.

"I'll go when I'm called."

"You won't be called!" half a dozen roared at once, and Moore added, "Long as you're good friends with Cap'n Robertson."

"I resent that!" shouted Shelby.

"Resent it and to hell with you!" said Jud Montague.

"He's gettin' fat from the war," said a voice from the back. "He prints legal notices from the Confederacy and gets paid in gold."

"I take my pay in Confederate paper like anybody else."

Talley began to feel uncomfortable, but the fat drummer, sitting in the front row, shook his head. "He's talkin' truth. If conscription is fair for one it's fair for all."

"He's big and he's strong," shouted B. B. Davis. "Why ain't he fightin' if they need soldiers so bad?"

Shelby began to lose his temper. "I won't stand here and be insulted by a bunch of Black Republicans!" he thundered.

"Then come down and fight, you lily-livered editor! Let's see if the pen is mightier than the sword!"

Shelby charged around the end of the table toward Mumpy Moore, who had challenged him. The audience suddenly rose like a batch of dough and began to move as a mass—some one way, some the other, those who were near enough going toward the door. B. B. Davis, his eyes glowing with the blaze of battle, started up the aisle to meet Shelby. Mumpy Moore, making his way to the aisle, stumbled over somebody's feet. Davis, about half as heavy as Shelby, went down sprawling, but over his body came a solid wave of men to hit Shelby. For a moment he fought back. Fists flew and heads cracked, then Shelby went down on top of Davis.

But already a counterattack had formed, led by Ned Hungerford and Jesús. The first man they encountered was John Reynolds, the blacksmith. He stood for a moment with his back toward the platform, clutching with his big fingers, swinging his huge arms, but they rolled over him like a tidal wave. The hall was filled with oaths. Fists cracked on skulls. It began to break up into individual hand-to-hand fights, with the two sides swaying back and forth.

Talley, completely cut off from the platform, saw an opening in the direction of the door and went over the chairs, with Helen Partridge fol-

125

lowing. There was nobody left at the door, and he slipped outside and held up a hand to her. "You'd better get back to the shop and lock yourself in."

"What about you?"

"I've got friends in there," he said. "They may need help." He listened to the shouts from the building, the heavy thump of hard-soled shoes and boots on the floor, the grunts of men hurt and men trying to hurt, and he felt the sudden heady call to conflict.

"I'll have to stay around and see how it comes out."

"Be careful. The success of our project—"

He knew what she was thinking about, and was reminded of the letter in his pocket. "You want to go through with the trip?" he asked.

"Yes."

"Within the next two or three days—as soon as possible—get a rig from Moore and drive to San Antone. Don't take any money with you, for it's outlaw country."

"I can protect myself," she said coldly.

He shook his head. "Mrs. Partridge, for a long time you've gotten by because you're a woman, and in the South a woman is considered a lady. But don't overestimate your strength. A man like Joe Cooper would break your neck with one hand."

"I hate you for that," she said.

"It took away a little of your self-confidence,

didn't it? It was aimed to. I've told you before that you're in a man's country and you're not able to compete with men on their own terms. Long as you pretend you're a lady, you can get along, but the minute you start taking the place of a man, somebody is going to give you an awful bump."

"What do I do in San Antone?" she asked.

"Find a Señor Andrés Díaz, a lawyer. Make arrangements to buy all the quinine we can pay for. Count on me for forty thousand. Find out when and where we can get it—probably in Monterrey or Chihuahua. Don't give him any money. We'll pay on delivery. Then get back— and tell nobody anything." Talley went on: "Robertson and his men are watching me like a hawk. A trip to San Antone would be a dead give-away for me, because that's smuggling headquarters. So I can't be connected with it until the last minute—when it will be too late for them to do anything."

"Wouldn't it be easiest for you to go to Robertson and tell him what you intend?"

"He might not believe me. Now get home and lock the door. I'll give you time to make the trip to San Antone, and I'll be back. When you arrange the delivery date, remember it will take twelve or fourteen days for us to get to Monterrey."

He watched her disappear in the darkness. Then he went back toward the hall. He left the path and followed the side wall of the building to the window nearest the platform, and looked through.

They had settled down to serious fighting inside. Two men lay inert on the floor, apparently unconscious, while three others were sitting up in corners or with the help of chairs, waiting to get their breath or perhaps strength to re-enter the fight. A small group of women huddled in the corner past the platform, unable to reach the door because of the conflict. The Reverend Garrison stood uncertainly at the edge of the platform, wiping his bald head with a bandanna and occasionally pleading for a cessation of hostilities. But his plea was addressed to no one in particular, and Talley thought it would be a disappointment to the Reverend if the fight did stop at his exhortation.

Adele had gone over to the group of women in the corner and was waving a tiny handkerchief under the nose of one who seemed to be struggling against a fainting spell.

The window was nailed tight, and Talley broke the glass with his elbow; the buckskin protected him from cuts. With his arm he raked out the jagged pieces still in the frame, put one leg through, and climbed inside.

Shelby was at the apex of a wedge trying to cut its way to the door with fists and knives and chair legs, but they were opposed by a bigger gang headed by the now hatless B. B. Davis, Mumpy

Moore, the husky John Reynolds, and Jud Montague, who was swinging a chair leg with the dexterity of much practice. All the lamps were still in place and undamaged.

Talley shouted at Adele but she did not seem to hear him. The shouts and curses and shuffles and stomps made too much noise, and even the Reverend didn't hear him, but stood on the edge of the platform looking confused but happy.

Talley ran forward but fell over the tangle of a demolished chair and landed hard on his face at full length.

He got to his knees, but a boot caught him under the chin and stretched him flat on his back. He had sense enough to roll, and Shelby's big feet landed where his face had been. He grabbed the man's leg and pulled him off balance long enough for his head to clear.

Shelby swore. "Try to sneak up on us from behind!" he growled as he got his balance.

Talley ducked a battering knee and came to his feet. Shelby, his face bloody, swung a chair leg at him. Talley jumped back and found himself in the corner, eight or ten feet from the women. He shouted at Adele, "Get out the window!" and faced Shelby. The man came at him. Talley braced himself against the wall and fought him off with his feet.

Adele had hold of her father's arm, trying to pull him toward the window. The chair leg cracked across Talley's instep. He grunted and his foot dropped, limp and numb. Adele and the Reverend were leaving the platform—but slowly, too slowly. If somebody knocked over one of those kerosene lamps, the place would go up like gunpowder.

The other women now began to trail across the floor to the broken window. As Shelby rushed him, Talley doubled up and rolled, but Shelby caught him in the small of the back with a boot, then fell over his rolling body. He jerked the chair leg from Shelby's fingers and started to swing it, then a swarm of men surged against him.

When they were through, he lay for a while, battered and bloody. The fight was still going on in the center of the room. The ladies were gone, either through the window or through the door. Talley got to his feet and made his way to the window. He got through, half-falling on his face outside.

He left the hall and went to Hancock's store, where his team was tied. He got the wagon turned around, and then a man stepped into the street from the front door of the hotel. In the dim light, Talley recognized an army hat. He pulled up on the reins, and Robertson came up and put one foot on the hub of the front wheel.

"What's been going on down there at the hall?" he asked.

"Just what it sounds like—a fight."

"Anything in particular?"

"Nothing but conscription."

He couldn't see Robertson's face, and so he couldn't tell how the man felt, but Robertson said slowly, "It's a waste of time to fight about it. It has already been decided."

Talley licked blood from his upper lip. "What do you mean?"

Robertson took a deep breath. "Gillespie County and part of Kerr have been declared in a state of rebellion, and will be placed under martial law. Texas belongs to the Confederacy, Talley, and starting tomorrow Texas men are going to fight like everybody else."

CHAPTER X

HELEN PARTRIDGE was up early the next morning. She made a quick breakfast of tea and dry biscuits, and walked through the dusty street to Moore's Livery Stable. Moore was forking out hay for the horses, and the stable smelled sour from the horses and sweet from the hay.

"Howdy, Mis' Partridge."

"I want a buggy and a good horse to go to San Antonio," she said.

He frowned and leaned on the fork handle. "Mighty long trip for a lady," he observed. "Might be safer takin' the stage."

She said quietly, "The stage doesn't run regularly—and it isn't safe. Do you want to rent a horse and buggy?"

"Yes, ma'am, I reckon I do. You can't make it in one day, though."

"I don't expect to."

"Most gener'ly they leave late in the afternoon and camp on the creek twelve miles out. You'll have to camp two nights instead of one, but—"

"I'm leaving now," she said.

"Two mighty long days' drive."

"Have you got a horse that will stand up to it?"

He looked around at the stalls and considered. "Well, I got a good bay mare over there. She don't look like much but she's pure mustang. She'll still be puffin' when your fancier horses have quit for good."

"I'll depend on your judgment."

He got the bay mare's halter and backed her out of the stall. "I better throw some corn in the back of the buggy. You'll be gone four-five days."

"I think so."

"Have to ask you fer a deposit."

She gave him two gold pieces.

His eyes lighted up when they saw the coins.

"Mind, I want that gold back," she told him. "I'm not trading for anybody's paper money."

He nodded, discouraged. "Yes, ma'am." He put the pieces in a pocket of his vest. "When you git to San Antone, drive to Los Caballos Livery and

132

tell 'em I sent you. They can take care of the rig if anything happens to you."

"Nothing will happen," she said. "Get the buggy."

He rolled it out and backed the mare between the shafts. He threw a tow sack half full of corn behind the seat. He put a whip in the socket and handed her the reins. "I'll help you up, ma'am."

"I can get up by myself."

She put one foot on the iron step and got into the buggy. She cracked the whip on the mare's back, and they were off.

She stayed in New Braunfels that night. It was a German town, and there was more heated talk about the war than there had been in Texas. She got a room at the hotel, ignored the tentative remarks of the drummers, and went to bed. She arose early the next morning, washed, and ate breakfast. She walked to the livery and had the mare harnessed up.

On the dusty road to San Antonio she began to feel the wildness of the country and the vulnerability of a lone traveler. Mile after mile of dusty road, with no human habitation, the undulating track of a rattlesnake across the road, buzzards circling in the distance over some dead or dying animal—all these appeared as omens to her and began to build up her fear as she watched in every direction for the approach of a horseman or a vehicle.

To get her mind away from it she thought about the men in Austin—Robertson, Talley, Shelby—each with his own problem and all of them important to her and her own success.

Robertson: he was of the gallant school of Georgians. She had encouraged his interest because he represented General Hébert and was in a position to do her either great good or great harm.

Talley she did not like. She never felt safe around him, for she never knew what he was thinking behind those steady blue-gray eyes, and she could never quite escape the feeling that he knew more about her than he let on. Talley was one man she couldn't endure very long under any circumstances, and as soon as she got her hands on the $40,000 she had plans for him.

Thinking about this, she took the derringer out of her reticule, saw that it was loaded, and laid it on the seat at her left side, where it would be in the shade of the buggy top.

Shelby was her kind, really—a big man, the biggest of the three, with a careless strength and a cynical look in his eyes that said he would hesitate at nothing to get what he wanted. If Shelby proved as ruthless as he seemed, she might learn to like him a great deal.

She had left the Guadalupe River at New Braunfels—a beautiful stream that ran over a hard white limestone bed and was bordered with very large pecan trees. She watered the mare in some holes in the bed of the Cíbolo, and there it was she saw a mounted man watching her from a distance.

The sight startled her, for the only mounted men who would watch her from a distance would be those who knew who she was—and nobody in this area knew who she was. It was possible some outlaw band had a spy in New Braunfels, but as she thought it over she felt sure she was being spied on by someone who had known the minute she left Austin—probably Cooper's men. She sat there in the buggy seat watching the mounted man from the corner of her eye while the mare drank. She tied a knot in the end of the reins and put her foot through; it left enough slack for her to hold the reins, but she would be able to turn loose of the reins and then recover them. She made sure the derringer was at her side, tried the whip to see if it was loose in the socket, and drove on.

She saw no one and met no one for a considerable time, but occasional drifting clouds of dust to the rear on her left side let her know that she was still under observation. She stopped at a small stream, the Salado, to rest the mare. She would have used the whip on the horse to keep going without rest, but she knew she might find herself afoot. She wondered why the man in the distance had not attacked sooner. Perhaps they wanted to have it happen near San Antonio.

She had traveled about ten minutes from the Salado when they closed in, one from each side. They came down from the prairie at a gallop, meeting her and pulling alongside. One man was black-haired, with several days' beard on his face, the other thin and brown and dried up. The black-haired one said, "Whoa! Pull her back there, lady!"

She pulled up slowly, trying not to show fear. Apparently they were not in a hurry. She let the reins drop on the dashboard, and her left hand at her side.

"Now hand over your money, lady, and we'll leave you go on your way," said the black-haired one.

She looked him in the eye. "I have no money," she said. "Cooper told you wrong."

His eyes narrowed. "Don't make trouble, lady, and there won't be no trouble."

"I have no intention of making trouble," she said, spotting the derringer from the corner of her eye.

He pulled closer and started to lean over. "Give me—"

Her left hand closed around the butt of the pistol and she shot him just above the right eye. The dried-up man, controlling his excited horse by savage jerks on the reins, shot at her, but she had pulled back in a corner of the buggy seat, and his shot went through the glass window in the rear. She snatched the buggy whip from its socket and swung it backhanded. The limber end wrapped around the man's neck, and the lash took skin off of his left cheek. She shouted at the mare and yanked on the whip at the same time, pulling him out of his saddle by the neck. Then the whip loosened and he fell into the road, while Mrs. Partridge kept low between the buggy seat and the dashboard and applied the whip to the mare.

Fifteen minutes later she looked back and saw there was no one in sight. She slowed the mare to a walk, and picked the pieces of glass out of the seat with fingers suddenly trembling from reaction, and threw them away.

It was evening when she reached San Antonio, rumbled over the bridge across the river in the middle of town, saw men and women bathing in the canals. She got a room at a hotel near Los Caballos Livery, freshened up, had supper, and sat in the lobby that night listening to the talk with her hands busy at embroidery and her eyes upon her hands.

Here she heard the Spanish language used as much as English, and the talk was all of goods, ammunition, profits, but if anyone was dealing in quinine, they were not talking about it. She went to bed well satisfied.

The next morning she awoke early, hearing a rooster crow, but she went back to sleep, for the sun was bright and warm, and nobody seemed to be stirring. When she awoke again it was mid-forenoon. From the hotel window she saw bathers splashing in the canal, dogs chasing children, hogs rooting in the garbage of the gutters.

At one-thirty she went out into the business district, only to find that most men were home taking a nap or having a nip. She went back to the hotel and waited as patiently as possible for another hour. Then she again carefully made her toilet and went out. She located a small one-story adobe that had the single word *"Abogado"* on the door in fancy lettering, and went in.

With the brilliant sun suddenly out of her eyes, she stopped just inside the door until the interior began to take shape. Then she saw the man.

He was leaning against the frame of an inner door. Every line of his body spelled indolence. He wore a brown, fuzzy, beaver hat—not as high as a tall hat, but pulled well down on his ears. He had no whiskers, but a thin mustache cut so short that it gave his mouth an appearance of dirtiness. He had a huge cigar in the middle of his mouth, with a long ash on the end. His lips were parted, and he held the cigar with two fingers on top of it, though this seemed to be more of a gesture than a necessity. His other hand was on his hip, the elbow out. Beneath the coat he wore a fancy black brocaded vest with golden fleurs-de-lis, and a heavy watch chain from one vest pocket to a buttonhole.

138

Her eyes went back to his face; that was what repelled her. His hair over his ears was bushy, and came down his cheeks in long, heavy side whiskers. His eyebrows were large but thin. He had a bold, massive nose, and as he watched her his eyes were slightly narrowed, with the under lids forming pockets, and the left side of his mouth was a little twisted until there was a deep crease that curved upward toward his nose. As he leaned against the doorframe, watching her, she saw the calculating cynicism of his eyes, and knew instinctively that this was no small-town *coyote;* this man was dangerous.

"I was looking for Señor Díaz," she said.

He moved away from the door. "Let us not be coy with each other, *señora.*" Vaguely she knew that his use of the word *"señora,"* without his knowing who she was, was a term of disrespect, but she was not concerned with that. "You have come to do business with a *coyote*—a clever man with connections. You do not care whether his name is Díaz or Williams or Bonaparte. You want something—and you will be able to get it if you can pay for it. What is it you want?"

She took a deep breath, "Quinine," she said.

He took the cigar from his mouth. "Not gun-powder or rifle castings?"

"Quinine," she repeated.

"It's obvious you have arrangements with the Confederacy to deliver the drug to them," he said, now rolling the cigar in his thick lips. "With a guaranteed market, you can afford to pay what it will cost to deliver it to you. There is considerable risk, you know, for the Union has spies everywhere—even in Mexico City."

"If the price is too high," she told him, "I may not be able to deal."

"If you were not able to deal," he said, "you would not have been sent here."

"Very well." She gathered her dignity—slowly under his cynical eyes, so like those of Hugh Shelby but so much more evil. "Where can you make delivery?"

He rolled the cigar in his lips. "Monterrey."

"That's too far from the border. There are outlaws, bandits, spies—" She shuddered delicately.

"You knew that before you came here," he said without moving his lips. "Do you want to take delivery in Monterrey at $20 an ounce, or do you want it in Laredo at $100 an ounce?"

"Twenty dollars an ounce!" she repeated. "I cannot think of—"

"It costs $8 in Mexico City. Do you expect the *arrieros* to haul it to Monterrey for nothing?"

"I don't expect to be robbed!"

He was not moved. "You'll sell it to the Confederacy for $200 or $300 an ounce—and you'll get gold."

"But twenty—"

"There is a Union consul in Monterrey, and he

has spies. I will guarantee delivery to you in Monterrey."

"How do I know you won't turn me in to the consul?"

"Why should I? He wants to see quinine taken to Texas as much as anybody."

"I don't understand."

"Because it drains gold from the Confederacy faster than anything else that can be bought." He was close to her, and his breath stank strongly of cigar tobacco. "How much do you want?"

She thought a moment. "Three thousand ounces."

He eyed her more closely, and now, she thought, his eyes were taking on a strange glitter in the semidarkness of the interior. "Give me $10,000 earnest money."

She smiled coldly. "There is no earnest money with a man like you. I will pay when I get the quinine."

"You're a likely looking woman," he said, taking the cigar from his mouth but not moving his eyes from her face. The stench of his breath and the goat-smell of an unwashed body came over her, and suddenly she was filled with loathing.

He put the cigar back in his mouth, directly in the center. "How long do you think you will last when I make up my mind?" he asked with a wolfish smile.

She slapped him hard on the cheek. The ash dropped from his cigar, and his eyes burned with a hardness that she never had seen before in anyone. She stalled continuation of this contest by asking coolly, "Whom do I see in Monterrey?"

He regarded her for a moment, his eyes hostile but otherwise unreadable. "There is a harness shop about a block from the U.S. consul's office. Inquire for the best saddler in Monterrey. His name is Don Agosto. Tell him you are very much interested in buying a genuine Guatemalan *aparejo*. Insist that it be genuine—and have the money with you."

"I'll be there August 24," she said.

"Very well, *señora*." He had leaned back against the doorframe, again mouthing his cigar. "I do not like to deal with a hypocrite, *señora*."

"What do you mean by that?"

"A woman does not get into the business of smuggling in times like these by being chaste."

She watched him warily now. This was something she understood in men. It was something she could deal with, but she knew instinctively that he was interested primarily in the money he could make by selling quinine at two or three times its cost. So she said coldly, "When I return, if everything is satisfactory, I shall see you again."

His grin was a leer. "I travel widely, *señora*. You may see me sooner than you think."

She went out without a word. He was still leaning in the doorway, indolent, smelly, evil by the very leathery texture of his skin. It was a relief to get into the sunlight again.

She went up one block and along a canal, listening to the light talk and laughter and the giggles of the young women bathing. She turned down a side street and saw a sign, "Druggist and Apothecary. Paints. Liquors. Groceries." She went in, maneuvering her wide skirt through the door by lifting it on one side. A young Mexican appeared from somewhere in the back and went out rapidly. She saw an old man with dirty glasses pushed up on his forehead; his wrinkled hands were flat on the wooden counter, and his skinny arms seemed to brace him up.

"Something?" he asked.

"I want some wolf poison."

"Strychnine?"

"Yes—if you please."

"Ten pounds?"

"Oh, no, not that much. A couple of ounces will be enough."

He said sharply, "You ain't got many wolves, ma'am, have you?"

"No," she said. "No, I haven't."

"Take half a pound to bait one carcass." He waited.

"Well, I—all right, I'll take a pound."

"It comes cheaper by the pound." He went into

the back room. She heard his footsteps, the tug-
ging of the lid from a small cask, a shuffling
sound as of a scoop in dry powder, and presently
he came out with a paper sack. "Mind you don't
get careless with that stuff, ma'am. It don't take
much to kill a man."

She stared at him for a moment. "How much?"
she asked.

"Oh, a piece the size of a small pea would do
the job."

"Thanks," she said.

"But for wolves," he went on, "you better be
more generous. Make slits in the carcass and drop
in half an ounce, then close up the cut and pull the
hide over it. It's best if you—"

She was already gone.

CHAPTER XI

TALLEY DROVE back home in good spirits. He
had had a fight and he was still whole. He sat
with his feet propped up on the footboard for a
while and sang to the team, but then he got to
thinking about the meeting that night and became
silent, trying to reconstruct the arguments.

The Reverend had said each state had a right to
decide for itself. If that was so, why not each
man? Why not choose up sides and let each man
do what he wanted? Wasn't that the idea behind
the whole thing—to allow individual freedom?

And yet that wasn't the entire answer either. Shelby had been right too: if every state stood by itself, they would all fall. There was more to the argument than met the eye.

The team splashed across the ford and settled into the collars for the long pull upgrade to the ranch house. Presently he saw a dim light from one window, and he knew his mother was using a precious candle to wait up for him.

He tied the reins to the seat-iron, leaving them loose enough to slap the rumps of the horses, and jumped down lightly and went to the creek. In the dark he felt for the saddlebags and assured himself they were still filled with gold. Then he caught up with the team, which had come to a stop, and drove them on up to the house, calling "Whoa!" loudly so his mother would not be alarmed.

The door opened a crack, and his mother asked, "Roy?"

"Yes, Ma."

His mother stared at him. "You've had a fight!" she exclaimed.

"Yes, Ma, a little one. I didn't get hurt, though."

He went back for the salt and coffee, and carried in the bags of meal.

He took in the calico last, and gave it to his mother. She unwrapped it, took it out of the brown paper, and held it to the candle. "Pretty!" she said. "A red and black design."

He unharnessed the team and turned them into the meadow, then went to the cabin.

He didn't awaken until late the next morning, when he heard the dogs baying a bobcat back in the hills.

"I've had breakfast," his mother said, "but I saved some batter for you."

He went down to the creek and washed his face, and went back to the house and combed his hair. He sat deep in the rawhide chair, warming his hands around the coffee cup.

"What's the news from Austin?" his mother asked.

"Lots of feeling," he said. "Meeting at the hall last night, turned into a fight."

"With you takin' sides," she said severely.

He grinned at her. "I said it was a fight, didn't I?"

"What about conscription?"

"It looks like we're going to have it. The Confederate captain told me last night they've declared martial law in Gillespie County."

"It's a shame," she said, unexpectedly fierce.

He looked up, astonished. "What's a shame?"

"That Texans have to be put under martial law to be made to do their share."

He considered. "How about Tom and Jim?"

"They came in yesterday for supplies. I tried to talk them into staying here, but they wouldn't."

She brushed her hair back over her ear. "I'd like to have one man in the family who would stay put."

"Maybe you've got one," he said, watching her flip the pancakes.

She did not answer for a moment. When she spoke, her voice was controlled and level, emotionless, as if she was afraid to say what she hoped. "I always thought you were dependable," she said cautiously.

"There's some things I don't understand about it, but I got it figured out this way: we've got a right to secede as a state. If so, we could secede from the Confederacy as well as we could from the Union, and the Confederacy will try to force us back in line just the same as the Union is doing now. The way I see it, that gives every man a right to secede from the state or county or whatever when he's a mind to. But that's just theory. Actually you need the power of a nation behind you, or some other nation will gobble you up." He pulled up to the table and pushed his hat back as his mother set six big pancakes in front of him. "The world is full of nations, and if you don't line up with one, another one will grab you."

"We're short on butter," his mother said as he picked up his knife. "The cow we got from Houston is getting ready to drop a calf."

"If we want to fight Indians," said Roy, "we don't do it one man at a time. We go by families.

The families get together and side each other. Pretty soon you have a whole state workin' together." He ate a few bites. "The one thing I don't know," he said, "is where it ought to stop. Maybe there isn't any special place. Maybe when you get up to the size of a nation it all depends on who's the strongest. But for now," he said, "it's the Confederacy, and if a majority votes to form a new republic here in Texas, I figure I'll fight for that too."

She took a deep breath. She was a faded woman with gray hair, but her eyes were shining. "I'm glad to hear you say that, Roy."

"I'm glad I got it off my chest."

She sighed. "Are you going to volunteer?"

"Maybe later—not just yet. Ma, do you know what is the one most important thing to the Confederacy right now?"

"Men, I suppose."

"Not men—quinine. And I'm going to Mexico pretty soon after it."

She nodded slowly at the stove. "Isn't it dangerous, going to Mexico?"

"Anything is dangerous," he said.

He felt pretty good. He had pleased his mother and he had satisfied his own conscience. He wondered how hard it would be to get that quinine over the border.

CHAPTER XII

HE WENT UP in the breaks to see his brothers, but they were determined and belligerent, and he did not try very hard to talk them out of leaving. He gave Tom a few pieces of gold, and got a sneer in return.

"You got a tubful of these," said Tom, tossing them up and watching them glint in the sunlight, "and you expect us to be satisfied with half a dozen." Tom turned his slant jaw sidewise. "When are we leaving Texas?"

"I'm not leaving."

Tom stared at him, his jaw outthrust. "What do you mean—you're not?"

"I've decided to stay and see it through."

"Well, I haven't," Tom said loudly. "You can stay if you want—but give us our share and we'll git."

"There's no call for dividing anything. The ranch will be here when you get back."

"We ain't comin' back."

Roy frowned. "You'll have to come back sometime." He saw Tom's hand on the butt of his pistol, and said sharply, "Don't pull that iron on me."

Tom's hand moved slowly away from the pistol butt. "You're actin' mighty bossy lately."

"And you're actin' like a coyote in a watermelon patch. You two been up here for months," said Roy, "doing nothing. You need some work to take the edge off."

"We choused out them cows for you to take to New—"

"That was January," Roy said impatiently.

"You was in favor of us stayin' hid out then," said Jim.

"I've changed my mind. I think you ought to go into Austin and act like men."

"I'm not goin' to make up to no Confederate enrollment officer," Tom argued.

"It's up to you. I told you what I thought."

He went back to the ranch and got to work on the corrals, to replace posts that had rotted under the winter rains or had been kicked down by the horses. He patched harness, killed a couple of bears for oil, and rode out through the breaks every few days to see how the cattle were coming. There had been a good crop of calves, and if the wolves didn't get too bold—but he was afraid there would be plenty of wolves, for there were lots of rabbits.

Sometimes he picked up a deer or a couple of wild turkeys, sometimes half a sackful of pecans. The plums, he saw, were going to be good if there was lots of sun, and they made nice plum cobbler and good jelly.

All of the sows but one had big litters of pigs, and there were three new colts. He carried his branding iron on his saddle, and occasionally when he got half a dozen new calves together, he made a fire and burned the R Bar T into their hides. Not that it made much difference, he thought. With New Orleans in Union hands, and with Unionists watching the Mexican border, there wasn't much a man could do with cattle anyway. Branding them, he guessed, was sort of a habit, but maybe some day the war would be over and there'd be a market for fat steers. Some of them might be ten-year-olds by that time.

His mother made candles with the wicking he bought in Austin, and she got out the spinning wheel, for cloth, even at smugglers' prices, was almost nonexistent by that time, and she set to spinning the yarn for the rough but durable material they had used for both men's and women's clothing back in Mississippi.

He decided to take twenty sides of bacon and a dozen hams into Austin to trade for supplies; he would have preferred to keep the meat in the smokehouse, but it attracted too much attention to drive into Austin with an empty wagon and out again with a load of scarce goods.

His mother said longingly, "I haven't been to town since last fall."

"Then get on your Sunday duds and we'll be movin'." He added, "Don't dress up too much."

She said slowly, "I haven't got anything to dress up too much in."

He finished harnessing up and drove to the door. His mother came out in her silk dress that was six years old, and a sunbonnet so faded that it didn't match any more.

They drove down the slope, Roy using the brake a little.

After a while she asked, "Roy, where do you go for this quinine?"

"To Mexico," he said, "and it's an absolute secret."

He hadn't meant it to, but the mention of Mexico sobered her, and he knew she was wondering about his father: where he was, what he was doing, if he was eating regularly, if he was warmly clothed. With the disruption of communications, they had had only two or three letters from the elder Talley since he had crossed the border.

He reached the bottom of the grade and stopped the wagon to breathe the horses. With his mother holding the reins, he went down to the river and found the saddlebags. He took half a dozen gold pieces from one of them, and strapped it shut. Then, thinking about Tom and his willfulness, he carried the saddlebags downstream to a point where he could not be seen from the house. He found a hollow tree where he had gotten honey a few years before, and carefully stowed the gold in that and covered it with brush. He cleared away his tracks, took the saddlebags to the creek and filled them with rocks, then took them to the original hiding place and slid them into the water.

When he got back to the wagon, his mother asked: "Taking care of the money, Roy?"

"Yes."

"You don't trust anybody, do you?"

"You," he said briefly.

"It isn't good to be so suspicious."

"It isn't safe not to be," he told her.

He stopped at the Garrisons', and Adele came out to meet them, smiling at his mother. "Mrs. Talley, it's good to see you again," she said as she hugged her.

"I've had lots to do on the ranch," Mrs. Talley said.

"Where's the Reverend?" asked Talley.

"He started for the post office—though I don't see what sense there is in it. There's no mail any more."

"I need to buy some things," Mrs. Talley said. "I thought you might like to go with me."

Adele said, "I'm glad to, Mrs. Talley, but there's mighty little to choose from. Could you wait until I get dressed up a little?"

"We've got plenty of time, haven't we, Roy?"

"Plenty," he said. He was watching the color come and go in Adele's white skin. If there was anybody besides his mother he could trust, it would be Adele. He remembered how she had gone hunting with him and his brothers before they were old enough to be aware of one another as boy and girl. She had been a tomboy then, and a good shot. She was a good shot yet, but she certainly had outgrown all evidence of boyishness. Decidedly. "Yes," he said, "there's plenty of time."

He took them to Hancock's and tied the team out in front. He looked first toward the millinery store, then at the print shop. It was a hot day, and Shelby was sitting in his front doorway, smoking. Talley changed his mind and went to the post office.

Halfway there he met Helen Partridge, immaculately dressed, black hair gleaming.

"Good morning, Mr. Talley. I haven't seen you in several days."

"Been pretty busy on the ranch." He pushed his hat back on his head. "Can't get help with the work any more."

She asked, "Is that your mother over there with Adele Garrison?"

He turned to look. "That's her."

"I've never met her," Helen Partridge murmured.

"I can't think of any reason why you shouldn't. Come on."

He walked with her to cut them off. "Ma, I want you to meet Mrs. Partridge."

His mother looked Helen over. No sign of feeling showed in his mother's eyes. "Are you staying in Austin long?" she asked.

"I hope to. I'm tired of the war. I had a husband in Lane's Rangers."

"Roy hasn't told me about that." His mother looked at the wagon, past Helen's shoulder, and said quietly, "We've many of us been left widows by the war."

It was a little strange, thought Roy, that Helen Partridge did not ask more about that. Instead, she said, "It is nice to have met you, Mrs. Talley."

Mrs. Talley looked at her and nodded. Talley could not tell what his mother was thinking, but her next words informed him. "Roy, what are we going to do for sweet'ning? Sugar's six-bits a pound, and I won't pay it. They say it comes from Mexico—but that's no reason for charging top prices. Somebody must be making a big profit."

"I've got a couple of bee trees spotted," Roy told her.

"And I couldn't even buy buttons or needles."

"I have a few needles I can spare," said Helen Partridge. "I'd be glad to let you have some." She observed Mrs. Talley's obvious hesitation without apparent feeling, and said cheerfully, "In a time like this, we all have to pull together, you know."

There were strong undercurrents among the three women that Talley did not altogether follow for the next few seconds; then his mother said, without smiling, "It is kind of you to offer, but I am not quite out. I will let you know when I need more."

"Please do that," said Mrs. Partridge. "And I hope both of you will feel free," she said, taking in Adele, "to look at my hats whenever you are interested in millinery."

His mother glanced at her but did not reply. "George Hancock said needles are being smuggled around the country at a dollar apiece," said his mother. "I declare. I can make buttons out of gourd seeds, but I don't know how to make needles."

"It's no wonder we can't fight a war," said Adele, "with everybody making such big profits."

Roy glanced at her. She was watching Helen Partridge from the corner of her eye, but whatever thoughts Mrs. Partridge may have had she kept to herself.

CHAPTER XIII

THEY SEPARATED. Helen Partridge went toward the hotel; Talley went into the billiard hall; and Adele and Mrs. Talley went toward Arnheim's store, undoubtedly to see if old Arnheim had any more of a stock than Hancock.

He spoke to men in the billiard hall, walked around the room, and went out again. He started for the saloon to have a drink, but on the way he passed the *Bugle* office. The windows were small and very dirty, and there was no sidewalk along the front of the building itself, so his flat-heeled boots made no sound. As he passed, he saw Helen Partridge inside. He paused for only a second, but in that time he saw her hand a folded piece of paper to Hugh Shelby. The editor was sprawled back in his chair, untidy and lazy as usual, but he reached for the paper at once.

While Talley idly wondered what was on the paper—perhaps it was wording for an advertisement or some such thing—he heard her controlled, clear voice say, "—in one-ounce packets."

He went on past the windows without stopping, but his lips were grim when he reached the board sidewalk beyond. Mrs. Partridge had told Shelby about the quinine! That meant one of two things: either Shelby was in with Cooper's gang and Mrs. Partridge was playing into his hands, or Shelby was a Confederate spy. Or perhaps—the thought struck him like a blow—Shelby was a Union spy.

Talley turned back toward the billiard hall. He had something to think about. The affair at Buass Hall had given some indication—if any was needed—that Shelby was mixed up with Joe Cooper's gang. Now Helen Partridge was dealing with Shelby.

He ordered half a dozen fried oysters to kill time. Actually, as far as he could see, it didn't make any difference whom she worked through, but just the same he didn't like her dealing with

Shelby. Coming like that, it was something of a shock.

He waited long enough to give Helen Partridge time to get back to the millinery shop; then he went over.

She had a mouthful of pins and was working on a hat. "I'm glad you're here," she said.

"Did you see the man in San Antone?"

She nodded. "The price is high, but we can make a thousand per cent—maybe more."

"Where and when do we get it?"

"We are to be in Monterrey August 24."

"How much did you order?"

"Three thousand ounces—in one-ounce papers packed sixteen to the tin."

He looked at her, remembering what she had said to Shelby. "How much an ounce?"

"Twenty dollars."

"All right. We'll leave here August 12."

"I think you said you know that country."

"I know half the Mexicans between here and there, and I know the brush country. You needn't worry about that, Mrs. Partridge. We'll have plenty of help if we need it."

She took the hat off the stand and held it at arm's length. It was light blue. "Do you think that's pretty?"

"Pretty enough—but are you going to leave all the pins in it?"

"The pins will come out after I sew it."

Adele would look good in that color, he thought, but he didn't suggest it. "I'm sorry," he said, "that Adele and Ma aren't more friendly. I guess they're worried about—things."

"It's all right," she said. "It was not unexpected—and not too important. It's the quinine that is important."

She put the hat on a peg in the wall in the middle of a dozen other hats, and backed off to look at it. "Miss Garrison has taken an obvious dislike to me."

He shrugged. "It's always that way when a new woman comes to town."

"I'm really not after any other woman's man, you know. It's only a few months since I was married myself."

"Yes."

"Captain Robertson told me just the other day that my husband was killed in a night raid against Stewart."

"Too bad," he said, and got up. He didn't know why she continued the story about a husband; he didn't know if she was married—or if she ever had been married. He wondered if she ever told the same story twice. "Have you notified the Confederate officials we'd have quinine for them?"

She nodded twice. "This very day—so that if for any reason they don't want it, they can let us know before we start."

That very day, he thought as he went out. Did that mean Shelby?

He was unwrapping the reins when Robertson walked across the street. "It's a good thing you're going home early," he said. "There's another meeting tonight at Buass Hall."

Talley asked slowly, "Why are you interested in what I do?"

Robertson looked pensive, "I'm interested in anything that will bring peace to the country and help us in the war."

"Are you?"

Robertson's answer was earnest. "You may not believe this, Talley, but I have hopes of seeing unity in Austin. As long as we are all in this, we'd better all stick together."

"We aren't all in it," Talley said flatly.

"I know that. Your father isn't."

"What about him?"

"Those who are gone—are gone. But those who try to leave in the future, will be stopped."

"By what right?"

"By the right of necessity. We cannot have our man power pouring out through Texas into Mexico."

Talley drove to the Garrisons'. Adele had the coffee on, and his mother and the Reverend Garrison were sitting in the kitchen.

Garrison put three tablespoonfuls of bourbon in his coffee. He started to lick the spoon, but caught himself, and used it to stir the coffee instead. "The old town is humming," he said importantly.

"In what way?" asked Talley.

"Every way. The Confederacy says Texas has got to get into the war with both feet. *Got* to!" he shouted.

"We voted to," said Mrs. Talley.

The Reverend glared at her. "I didn't!"

Talley asked, "How far are they going with this enrollment?"

"As far as necessary, Robertson says." The Reverend drank about half of his coffee. "It ain't Robertson himself, exactly—he's a peaceable man, far as I see—but there are others who are bound to make us fight if they have to whip us to do it."

"What about my boys?" asked Mrs. Talley.

The Reverend glanced at Roy. "He'll be exempt, but them two in the hills—they'll go after them."

"Jim isn't sixteen," said Mrs. Talley.

"Tom is."

"He's nineteen," she said, looking down.

The Reverend shook his finger at her. "They aren't going to be easy on them who hide out. I'll promise you that!"

They had a silent ride home, with the empty wagon rattling behind a team eager to reach the corral and get a feed of corn. It was dark when they pulled up the long slope. The wagon clattered over the outcropping of limestone and they swung around behind the house.

After his mother went in, he unhitched the horses and took them to the barn. He wondered if the meeting that night would break up in a fight.

CHAPTER XIV

THE NEXT morning he put a blanket and saddle on the *bayo* and rode away up the river. It was almost the first of July, and the plum bushes were loaded with hard, green fruit. Wild grapevines were beginning to show dusty purple clusters, and the sides of the *arroyadas* were dotted with blue-green cedar trees.

He found the cave where the boys had been. The fire was out and the ashes scattered by swirls of wind; the boys had been gone for some time. He found the two saddlebags, both empty of the rocks he had put in them. The sun had dried them out, and the leather was stiff and hard. He picked them up and threw them behind the *bayo's* saddle. Then he took the reins and walked upstream, looking for tracks. He found where they left the valley and went through a dry wash, cutting west toward the Pedernales River.

He rode back home, getting there about noon. His mother had baked a ham and made corn dodgers, and he ate almost greedily.

"What about Tom and Jim?" asked his mother, watching him.

"They went west," he said. "I figure they were headed for Bear Creek in Gillespie County."

She said in a troubled voice, "They're going to fight the Confederacy?"

He took more ham. "I don't think so, Ma. I think these companies are organized to get out of joining the army. Some of the young fellows might act belligerent, but I don't think the older heads would be foolish enough to organize a rebellion."

"A rebellion within a rebellion," his mother murmured. "Is there to be no end to it?"

"It's not easy to answer," he said. "The Confederacy isn't going to like it."

"What can they do about it?"

"Send soldiers to break it up."

She said with a deep sigh, "What would happen to those found on Bear Creek?"

"They probably will take them into the army. At least, I think that's the way they will figure." He got up suddenly. There was apprehension in her quick glance. "Where you going, Roy?"

"To Austin. I've got to find out what the talk is. If this is a big movement, and if the Confederate officials are going to do something about it, I want to be with them. Maybe I can save some trouble for those on Bear Creek."

It was early Sunday evening when he got to

Austin. The Reverend Garrison was filling the kerosene lamps in Buass Hall. Talley stepped in. "What's the talk, Reverend?"

The preacher screwed the brass assembly back into the glass base of a lamp. "There's more talk than I could tell in a month," he said, "but mainly it's about the Union Loyal League."

"What about it?"

The red-faced, roundheaded preacher wiped kerosene from the fingers of his left hand with a rag. "You know they organized about a year ago, and they've been recruiting ever since."

"Not to fight the Confederacy."

"Do the Confederate officers know that? What would *you* do," he demanded, "if you were in command of the Department of Texas, and several hundred men met in one spot?"

"I'd sure keep an eye on them."

"So would I."

"What's the meeting for tonight, then?"

"Mostly, I think, a prayer meetin'—anything to convince the Confederates we aren't planning an uprising."

Garrison had changed his tune, Talley thought. At the post office the hitching poles were loaded with an unusual number of saddled horses. He looked over the brands and went up to Captain Robertson's office. "What is your idea about this meeting in Gillespie County?" he asked.

Robertson's face looked drawn. "Officially I

don't know anything about it because it's out of my county, and spying is not a part of my duties anyway. But unofficially I can say that the Confederacy will not look on it with any kindness." He found a cigar in his desk. "Have one?"

"No thanks. What will they do about it?"

"If it were my responsibility," Robertson said, striking an evil-smelling sulphur match, "I would take steps to break it up."

"It isn't illegal, is it?"

"Lots of things can be illegal at a time like this." Robertson looked at him. "Your two brothers are on the way to Bear Creek, aren't they?"

Talley was thunderstruck. "How did you know? They just left yesterday."

Robertson's eyebrows raised. "Afraid I talked out of turn. Just trying to save some trouble for your family."

"What do you care? You have no kin in Texas."

"I have parents and brothers and sisters and even children, back home in Georgia. It's a town something like Austin, and I keep thinking, what if the war comes to that town?" He looked long at Talley. "I think of those things, and I try to temper my actions accordingly, but you must remember one thing. I am an officer in the Confederate army. I have certain duties to perform, without regard to my personal feelings. I wish the people of Austin would understand that. It would save a great deal of trouble."

"I don't think the men in Gillespie County mean to offer armed resistance to the Confederacy."

Robertson studied him. "Any large gathering of men might easily be construed as a threat to the established goverment."

"Tegener is leading them, and he's not a military man," said Talley. "He is a peaceful citizen who operates a sawmill."

"The man who runs a sawmill can also pull the trigger of a rifle," said Robertson.

Talley said stubbornly, "It is men like Captain Duff in San Antonio who present a more serious threat to peace."

"What do you know about Duff?" asked Robertson.

"I know he's a professional soldier, dishonorably discharged from the Union army. He believes that force should rule. His men pillage and loot, and they say that in his capacity as military ruler of some counties he has hanged men without a legal trial. I don't like to think of him leading armed men into the camp on Bear Creek."

"There's just as much danger of trouble here in Austin."

"How do you mean?"

"Take Jud and Eph, the town loafers," said Robertson. "It is their kind that helps to fan the flame of violence."

"Why don't you arrest them?"

"I can't. They're too shrewd to do anything you can put your finger on." Robertson flicked the ash from his cigar. "The leaders in affairs like this are often men without any loyalty and without any strong feeling except that of doing violence."

"You mean they're rabble-rousers?"

"Something like that."

"I think," said Talley, turning it over in his mind, "that I should go out to Bear Creek and try to show these men that what they're doing is dangerous."

Robertson glanced at him sharply. "It's worth while to try."

Talley said decisively, "I'll leave in the morning."

Robertson said, "I'll notify General McCulloch at San Antonio that you're going, so that if anything happens you will not be taken for one of the insurgents."

Talley paused. "It's serious then, isn't it?"

"Very serious," Robertson said soberly.

CHAPTER XV

HE SWUNG into the saddle and left town at a lope. At home he stopped and got a saddlebag full of parched corn.

"I may be gone a few days," he told his mother. "I'm going out to Bear Creek."

"I wish Tom and Jim would come back," she said soberly.

"I'll try to persuade them."

"There's not much you can do with Tom. He's awfully stubborn."

"Maybe I can talk to some of the leaders." He swung into the saddle and turned the *bayo* upstream.

That night he stayed in the cave, with the *bayo* staked out on the flat below. By sunrise he was following the course of the Pedernales, riding the ridge on the north side. He heard coyotes singing, but it was fair weather and they were truly *cantando*. He felt safe for the time being.

He rode hard that day, and a few hours after dark he saw fires reflected against the sky. Within half an hour he came upon a flat where hundreds of men were camped. There was nothing warlike about the gathering except that there were so many of them. He rode through on horseback, finding his brothers at the far end watching two men, stripped to the waist and with their left arms tied together at the shoulder, testing each other at Indian wrestling. He called, and Tom came over, at once surly and aggressive.

"What are you doin' here?" Tom demanded.

"I came to talk to the commander."

There was a ring of men around them already, and the two Indian wrestlers stopped to watch.

"What business is it of yours?" asked Jim.

"Maybe it's none. That's why I want to talk to your commander."

"We haven't done anything," said Tom.

"You've got rifles, haven't you?"

"Sure," said a black-bearded young giant in a nasal drawl. "You didn't expect to ketch us naked, did you?"

The men guffawed.

"Where is Major Tegener?" Talley asked.

"What are you—a damn Secessionist spy?" asked the young giant.

Tally turned on him coldly. "It doesn't take a spy to find a trail herd. Where's Tegener?"

"Up there under the trees," somebody said.

By now the whole camp was beginning to move toward a small fire under a tall pecan tree. Talley called, "Major Tegener?"

A man stood up. "I'm Fritz Tegener. What do you want?"

Talley leaned on his saddle horn. "I want to talk."

"Get down."

He scrutinized Talley, his eyes pausing at the six-shooter on Talley's hip, the rifle in the saddle scabbard. He was a big man, typically German and not, thought Talley, a man to take unnecessary chances.

"Take his horse to the guard," Tegener said, and a man appeared out of the darkness to take the reins and lead the horse away. "Now—did you give your name?"

"I'm Roy Talley from Austin. A couple of my brothers are with your—company."

"Sit down. Coffee?"

"It would taste good," said Talley.

"Bergmann, get a cup."

Talley glanced up at a big, florid-faced man with shifty blue eyes. He met Talley's gaze for a moment and then turned away. A moment later he handed Tegener a tin cup, and they all sat down except Bergmann—five of them now around the fire, Bergmann standing. The coffee was bitter, and Tegener apologized for not having sugar. The men who had followed Talley to the fire began to drift away.

"Major," said Talley, "I rode through your entire camp without being challenged."

Tegener smiled. "This is not a military organization and we are not here to do any fighting."

"How many men you got?"

"About five hundred."

"What are you doing here?"

"It is very simple. We are men who do not want to fight against the Union."

"That means you are willing to fight against the Confederacy."

"By no means." Tegener smiled again. "We are neutral. Can you ask for more than that?"

"What I ask," said Talley, "is of no importance. What the Confederacy asks may be altogether different."

"They can't force us to fight if we don't believe in it."

"I wouldn't bet on that," said Talley.

"Nevertheless, we are not fighting men. We oppose conscription, but we are not taking arms on either side."

"Have you ever thought how it would look to General Hébert when five hundred able men gather in a place like this—and especially in Gillespie County where Union feelings are strongest?"

"We have thought of that, but" Tegener insisted, "we are not fighting men."

Talley looked at him over the tin cup. "Then why do they call you 'major'?"

He saw the German's face swell with sudden suspicion. "Are you working for the Confederates?" Tegener demanded.

"No. I'm working to keep men from being killed."

Tegener studied him suspiciously, "We organized, yes. We have three companies—one for each county: Gillespie, Kerr, and Kendall. Each company naturally has a captain, and I have been elected major of them all. We also have chosen an aavisory board, and intend to do nothing that will disturb the peace."

Talley finished his coffee and put down the cup. "I wish I could be as calm about it as you are, major, but I can't."

"Why not? We are assembled peace—"

"If it is peaceable, then why are Confederate spies among your men?"

Tegener chuckled. He reached for a twig to

171

light his pipe. "No spies," he said. "There's nothing here to spy on."

Talley said heatedly, "This meeting was known to Confederate officers in Austin yesterday afternoon!"

Tegener looked startled. Then he puffed at his pipe. "Perhaps they heard a meeting had been called."

"No. They knew the men were here."

Tegener looked at the men around the fire. "What do you think, Kuechler?"

Kuechler said, "I don't know."

"I'm from Kerr County," said Hartman. "I'm not sure my men would break up even if we ordered it."

Tegener said thickly, "We agreed at the beginning that we would not maintain the battalion in the face of Confederate soldiers."

Talley said quietly, "You called it a battalion."

Tegener glared at him. Hartman said uneasily, "We planned to disperse anyway. Maybe we had better do it right away."

Tegener asked Talley, "Where did you get this information?"

"From Captain Robertson."

"That means," Kuechler said in a low voice, "that there is a spy in the battalion."

"That's what I'm trying to tell you," said Talley. "But that's not all. If one of your men is a spy, and is sending back reports, he may make them

172

sound the way he thinks the Confederate officials want them to sound."

Tegener turned it off. "Nobody would do that. There's no reason—"

"Anything can be a reason," said Talley. "It depends on the man."

"He's right," Kuechler said. "But who could it be? All of my men are from Gillespie County and are known to me personally or vouched for."

Talley kept silent. Finding the spy was their problem.

They talked it over, and the conservative German temperaments became alarmed. Finally the board voted to disperse the men.

"So you will see this is legal," Tegener told Talley, "come with me. Bergmann, tell the men to gather for a meeting."

The word went out through the valley, and the men stopped their games and began to drift toward the clump of pecan trees.

Tegener stood up. "Gentlemen, we have decided in the interest of peace to disband." A murmur arose, but he held out his hands. "We agreed to come here in peace."

The black-bearded young giant shouted, "We came to fight!"

"No, we did not meet to fight. We are protesting against conscription."

"We met in peace," Tom Talley said harshly. "We can stay in war."

"No," Tegener said, becoming alarmed. "It is insurrection. The Confederates will send soldiers to put it down."

A third man spoke up. "It's just choosing the side we're going to fight for."

"Gentlemen!" said Tegener. "We have already been reported to the authorities. There is a spy among us."

"If we ketch him," Tom Talley said, "we'll hang him."

There was a roar of approval.

"We don't know who it is," Tegener reminded them.

"We'll find him!"

"No inquisitions." Tegener was firm. "It is best we disperse at once. You will hear from me when the advisory board feels it is necessary to take further action."

There was considerable grumbling from the younger men, but other officers spoke and reminded them that their avowed purpose was to avoid fighting, and presently the meeting began to break up. The men returned to the burned-down campfires, now only glowing piles of coals, and sat around, smoking and talking.

Tegener said to Talley, "For a little while they had me scared."

"Sure," said Talley. "They didn't all come here with the same thing in mind as you. Some of them thought there would be fighting. Others came for the adventure of it. It's a safe bet there aren't twenty men in this valley who gathered here solely as a protest against conscription."

"At any rate," said Tegener, "we will scatter before any harm is done."

"If there is any harm," Talley said, "it is done already."

The camp was stirring the next morning as soon as the first light showed on the eastern horizon. Men poured down the valley to get their horses, and two hours later Talley, on the *bayo,* stopped beside Tom and Jim, who were on foot. "I'll ride along with you if you don't mind," he said.

Tom glared at him. "Who the hell do you think you are, bustin' things up? We was just havin' a good time."

"At the risk of your lives."

Tom's neck reddened. "What gives you the right to know everything?"

Talley said quietly, "You're a fool if you don't think five hundred men in one camp would attract attention."

Tom took a step toward him. "I tole you I wouldn't take any more off of you," he said, and seized Talley's right leg.

Talley slid out of the saddle and came down fighting. Tom was a little taller, but they were about the same weight. Talley lit into him with both fists pumping and knees and elbows working. By the time he got to the ground, Tom was falling back. Talley went after him. Tom brought up a hard knee and caught him in the groin. He doubled and fell over, and Tom had him by the throat.

Talley rolled. His eyes were going black. He took a last look at Tom's face and saw the fury there, and hesitated no longer. He snatched the six-shooter from his holster, reversed it, and brought the gun butt down on Tom's head.

Tom's fingers lost their strength. Talley hit him again. Tom's scalp was flowing blood. His arms dropped. Talley got up, breathing hard, and put the six-shooter in his belt holster.

The black-whiskered young giant stepped out. "Do you think you can lick me?"

Talley said briefly, "I think so," and waited.

The man glanced at the six-shooter and started to say more but changed his mind. Talley swung into the saddle and the *bayo* whirled to face downstream. Talley stopped it. "Tom, are you coming home?"

Tom was getting to his feet. "Hell, no!" he shouted. "Do you think I'd go home to be kicked around by you?"

"You'd be a lot safer than where you are."

"I'm goin' to Mexico," Tom said, and looked at Jim. "You're goin' too, ain't you, Jim?"

Jim nodded, not entirely sure, Talley saw, but not willing to go against Tom.

But Talley was tired of wet-nursing a couple who wanted to be mossyhorns—even if they were his brothers. He said, "You better keep out of sight, and don't go joining up with any big companies."

"We'll do as we damn well please!" shouted Tom, and Talley knew he would.

He cut across country to avoid the ranch, and pulled into Austin late that night. Robertson was sitting in the lobby of the hotel, and Talley sat down beside him.

"I wanted to tell you what I found out," Talley said, "because it may save some trouble for both sides. I found the meeting—about five hundred men, and I talked to Major Tegener and the advisory board. I pointed out to them that five hundred armed men were likely to be taken for fighting men."

"What did Tegener do?"

"The board voted to disband. When I left, they were breaking up."

Robertson thought about it. "You've done a good piece of work, Talley. I'll send a report to McCulloch immediately. If they have contemplated any action, this ought to stop it until they have time to investigate."

"From what I hear about Duff, it wouldn't stop him."

Robertson looked troubled. "Let's hope Duff is not on the way to Bear Creek."

CHAPTER XVI

TALLEY FOUND the answer to that the next morning when he heard harsh voices. He was out of bed in one leap, and in two more had flung open the door.

The sun was just showing through the pecan trees on the east. Chickens were clucking as they scratched in the grass, and the humming of bees came from across the meadow. But there were five saddle horses at the far corner of the cabin. A dismounted man held their reins. Two men with pistols were by the horses, and a fourth man was halfway to the door. A fifth man, a big, bristly, red-haired man in a gray Confederate uniform with the three bars of a captain, stood near the open door of the other cabin. And Mrs. Talley uncompromisingly held a rifle pointed at his stomach.

"Take your soldiers and get away from our land," she said, "if you don't want this thing to go off."

The officer looked at Talley. "I'm Captain Duff of the Partisan Rangers," he said. "Will you tell this woman to point that rifle somewhere else?"

Talley looked at Duff. "'This woman,'" he said, "is my mother. She was brought up in Texas and she has learned to hold a rifle on anybody who trespasses on her property."

"His corporal was in the hogpen," Mrs. Talley said. "That's how I heard them."

"Cap'n Duff," said the man holding the horse. "I know this woman. Her husband is in Mexico."

Duff grinned sardonically. "What do you say to that, Mr. Talley?"

Talley looked at him without changing expression. "I say you're a fool if you don't think my mother can shoot straight."

"We can rush you," Duff said.

"If you really thought so," said Talley, "you would have done it before now. Tell your men to get moving."

Duff glowered at him. Finally he muttered without turning his head, "Get on your horses."

The troopers stared at him, then slowly mounted.

"Now can we talk without that rifle pointing at me?" Duff growled.

"The floor is yours," said Talley.

"You've got lots of hogs," said Duff. "We need bacon and ham for the soldiers in San Antonio."

"It is for sale at a fair market price, provided you behave yourselves as gentlemen should."

Duff seemed to swell up. "Meaning what?"

"In Texas," said Talley, "when a man wants to buy pork he comes to the door like an honest man and says what he wants."

He saw that Duff was getting dangerously angry, but he wanted one thing impressed on the officer's mind. "Your man is lucky he isn't dead."

"General McCulloch has given me orders to forage."

"But not to pillage. How many hogs do you want, Captain?"

"Twenty head or more for now."

Talley said, "You have men in your company who are able farmers, haven't you?"

"Undoubtedly."

"Then send them here with the proper requisitions, and they can do the butchering."

"We are soldiers," said Duff, "not meat cutters."

"And I am a rancher," said Talley. "The only able-bodied man on the place, incidentally, and without time to kill hogs for the army."

Duff's bulldog lower jaw worked a little. "Talley, you are insolent and nonco-operative. I shall so report to General McCulloch."

"Do that," said Talley, "and tell him you tried to take my hogs without asking."

Duff looked from Talley to his mother, then back to Talley. When he spoke, he sounded conciliatory. "We haven't had anything to eat today, and I will pay you in gold for breakfast for my men."

Talley was about to assent when his mother spoke up. "Nobody eats in our house when they enter the way you did. Get on your horses and get off our land."

Duff stared at her, and then looked at Talley.

Talley raised his eyebrows. "You heard the verdict, Captain; it's only eight miles to Austin." He looked down the slope. The sun was in sight now over the pecans, and the deep grass on the slope was silvery with dew. "A couple of hours—" He stopped, staring at the grass. Then he looked at Duff. "You didn't come in from Austin," he said accusingly.

"No."

"Then you came down along the river."

"Yes."

"Why?" Talley demanded.

"I—"

"Were you trying to surprise my brothers—sneaking in the back door?" Talley asked harshly.

Duff hesitated before answering. "It is part of my duties to look for men evading conscription."

Talley's indignation showed itself in contempt. "You're lucky that you weren't shot," he said bluntly. "Now get on your horses and get away from here."

The men mounted slowly. Duff circled his white horse and stopped in front of Talley. His anger was almost out of control. "You will regret this summary treatment of me and my men, Talley."

"I regret," said Talley, thinking of the stories he had heard about Duff, "that such a man as you was ever accepted as an officer in the Confederate army."

There was work to do, for the trip to Monterrey would keep him away from the ranch for over three weeks, and his mother would be alone. Then one morning he left a wagonload of corn at the mill, and stopped by to see Adele.

She gave him coffee, and poured some for herself.

He cupped his hands around the coffee. "You're a mighty pretty girl," he said.

He watched the color rise into her throat and on to her face.

She started to answer, but there was a heavy knock at the front, and Adele hurried to the door. Talley heard a man's voice. Then Adele reappeared in the kitchen, bringing Captain Robertson, who carried his gray campaign hat in his hand.

"Good morning, Talley," he said.

Talley was trying to take this in. "Morning, Captain."

Adele seemed to be a little flustered, he thought. "Do sit down, Captain. I'll pour you some coffee."

"Thanks." Robertson sat straight and crossed his legs to balance the cup and saucer on his knee. "I hear from Miss Garrison," he said, "that you have plenty of hog meat on your place."

"Plenty," said Talley, "but it's all on the hoof. Know where I can get somebody to help butcher?"

Robertson looked at his cup, then at Adele, and back at Talley. "Isn't there any chance of getting your two brothers to come in peaceably?" he asked.

Talley took a deep breath. "They're young," he said, "and stubborn. I think they'll come if you give them time."

"Time is running out, Mr. Talley. Men are going hungry for lack of beef and pork that is plentiful in Texas, while Texas men are off cavorting around in public meetings."

"The men on Bear Creek went home," Talley reminded him.

"I wish *all* of them had gone home."

Talley looked up. "I thought they did."

Robertson shook his head sadly. "At least a hundred are still there. Gillespie County has again been declared in open rebellion, and Captain Duff has been ordered to restore peace and arrest the leaders."

Talley sat up straight. "Duff, did you say?"

"Yes."

Talley finished his coffee and said, "Thanks, Adele. I'll be going on uptown."

Robertson looked at him speculatively. "No need to hurry. I can't stay long."

Talley went on out. He didn't like Robertson's calling on Adele. He went over to the post office. There was no mail but the *Bugle*. He leaned idly against the bulletin board and scanned the front page. One inconspicuous paragraph said:

"Fredericksburg.—The three companies recently organized in Gillespie County have been disbanded, but Major Tegener has invited all Unionists who do not want to serve in the Confederate army to meet him on Turtle Creek in Kerr County, whence they will proceed to Mexico. It may be expected that the Confederate authorities in San Antonio will have something to say about this bald-faced evasion of duty."

Talley pushed his hat back on his head. Where had Shelby gotten such information as this? This was later than Robertson's information about Duff.

He folded the paper and put it under his arm. He went over to the billiard hall and had a glass of beer.

"Duff's men are pillaging Gillespie County," a man said at his side. "I heard that straight. They're takin' everything movable and some things that ain't."

"I'm glad I've got no wife and daughters over there," said a second man.

CHAPTER XVII

HELEN PARTRIDGE left her shop and went out on the street. She stopped in at the *Bugle* office, but Shelby wasn't there, the printer told her. "Left town yestiddy morning, and I don't look for him back ontil tomorrow."

"Did he say where he was going?" She accumulated all the information she could as a matter of course.

"No, ma'am—but I think he rode out west."

That would be in the direction of Gillespie County, where all the trouble was brewing.

"Is this my pile of exchanges?"

"I reckon so, ma'am. Least, he won't want 'em." He tied them with a piece of string.

"I'll save them—if he should want to see them again."

"It won't be necessary, ma'am. There'll be a new batch in tomorrow if the mail comes through."

She took the exchanges back to the millinery shop, and went through them one at a time, looking especially for items about malaria, chills and fever, or ague. She added up the number of mentions in her mind. It came to a hundred and twelve. The week before it had been only ninety-nine; the week before that, ninety-three. She was well satisfied. By the first of September the demand for quinine would be compelling, and the Confederacy would not be in position to offer objection to whatever price she might ask.

She had seen Roy Talley go into the billiard hall; now he came out and stood idly on the wooden walk, looking toward her place. He saw her in the door, and came across the street. He pushed his hat back on his head, and glanced at the pile of quarter-folded papers. "Catchin' up on the news?"

"I was interested in quinine."

"How's it look?"

"Better every week."

"Does anybody in Austin know about our trip?"

"Captain Robertson has tried to inquire—but I can handle him," she said.

He wondered if she would be so sure of herself if she knew that Robertson had gone to see Adele Garrison that morning. Maybe Robertson was a slicker customer than he let on. Talley got up. "We'll leave here the evening of the twelfth."

"Evening?"

"Yes. I'll bring my pack mules to carry the gold to Monterrey. That means we won't have to kill time buying animals to come back, too."

"We'll go armed, I assume."

He looked at her impersonally. "I'm sure you will, Mrs. Partridge—and I will too. I can put up a pretty good scrap, but you better remember one thing: from here to Monterrey the country is filled with men just as good fighters, and maybe better—and lots more of them. It'll take considerably more than brute force to get us there and back."

"I'm sure you will manage it."

"I expect to. You see Moore this afternoon and tell him you want a good saddle horse to take you to—say, Nacogdoches and back. The twelfth will be Tuesday. Be ready to leave the livery at sundown, and have your money with you."

"I'll be ready," she said.

As soon as the paper was out, Hugh Shelby had hired a horse at the livery and ridden out toward Fredericksburg. He didn't like to leave at a time like this, but he didn't see any way out of it. San Antonio was demanding information on Tegener's activities, and the only way to get it was to go after it.

He found some twenty-five or thirty men camped down along the stream, and sat his horse back in the trees while he looked them over. Two men were shooting at a mark, and two others were racing scrubby broomtails in a fiat near the creek. In the small crowd he recognized Tom and Jim Tallcy, and was glad he had been cautious. That Tom Talley was an ornery cuss to deal with when he got off on the wrong tack.

He saw a jug passed around, and Tom Talley took a good healthy pull from it, holding it on his left arm like a veteran. Jim passed it up.

It was mid-afternoon. The sun was hot, and big blueflies buzzed around the trees—perhaps because of refuse from the camp. His horse stamped at the flies and switched its tail, and Shelby led it deeper into the trees. He circled the camp and approached it from the upper end.

With his horse safely staked out half a mile away, he sat behind a screen of bois d'arc and studied the layout until he was familiar with every man in the camp. He could afford to be patient and thorough, for the Confederate quartermaster general had been generous with his official printing. Likewise they saw to it that he had newsprint. Where other editors around the state were having trouble printing at all, Shelby was making a very good profit.

Presently a man left the camp and headed for the trees, and Shelby moved to meet him. He stepped on a dry stick, and the man looked up in alarm. He was a big, florid-faced man, and for an instant he seemed about to turn and run, but Shelby said in a low voice, "Steady, Bergmann."

"Oh, Shelby!" He seemed relieved. "You scared me."

"Who you expecting—General Hébert?"

"No, I—they sent word that Captain Duff is coming up here—and I know him."

Shelby nodded toward the camp. "How do the men feel?"

Bergmann shrugged. "Nothin' special. They're hangin' around because they don't want to go home."

"Have you told them Duff was coming?"

"No. I was waitin' for orders."

"Are they getting ready to go to Turtle Creek?"

Bergmann looked down at the camp. "I've held

them back. I thought I'd better wait to hear from you."

"All right," said Shelby. "Now here's your orders. Get these men out of here tomorrow morning and join up with Tegener. Duff will come in here to Gillespie County and make a big fuss. Encourage Teneger to head for Mexico. Joe Cooper will keep in touch with you and find out how it's going. Duff will follow Tegener toward Mexico, but he won't attack him until he reaches the Nueces River. Got that?"

"Sure, but what about me when Duff attacks?"

"When the attack comes, you slip off into the brush and head for Mexico. Nobody will bother you."

"What about Tegener and the rest?"

"They're not your lookout. Do what you're told."

Bergmann's pale blue eyes fastened on Shelby's. "He aims to make an example out of them, don't he?"

"I don't read the minds of the generals or colonels. I follow orders. You better do the same."

Bergmann asked bluntly, "When do I get paid?"

Shelby took two gold pieces out of his belt. "There's forty dollars. That ought to carry you to the border."

"The deal was eighty," said Bergmann, reaching for the money.

"Maybe you don't know, but gold is mighty scarce, even in Texas."

Bergmann looked at the coins. "It isn't much," he said.

"It's more than I'm making out of it," said Shelby. Which was a lie, but he knew Bergmann would accept it.

Bergmann did brighten a little but tried at once to hide it. "All right, I'll move the men out in the morning. Then I'll keep the major headed towards Mexico, and I'll see Cooper often enough to report to him if there's any change."

Shelby nodded, his eyes half-closed. "You better get back down to the camp and start the boys toward the Nueces."

Bergmann kept fingering the two coins in his big hand; obviously he wanted to talk more about the money, but Shelby looked stonily at him. Bergmann dropped his eyes. Finally he turned and went back down the slope, wrapping the coins in a piece of buckskin and putting the little package inside of his shirt.

Shelby drew back deeper into the trees and made his way to his horse. He rode out along the ridge, keeping in timber for several miles. Presently he hit a trail and cut south a little. At the small settlement of Blanco he stopped at the grocery store. The mixed odor of kerosene and whisky was strong. He asked the storekeeper, "Can a man send a letter from here?"

The storekeeper sounded like a Yankee. "Horseback mail goes to New Braunfels once a week."

"What day?"

The storekeeper glanced at a calendar. "Tomorrow."

"Got any paper?"

The storekeeper shook his head. "No tablets, mister. Loan you a piece of wrapping paper."

"How about an envelope?"

"Cost you another five cents."

"All right."

"*And* two bits to get the letter carried."

Shelby scowled. He tossed a silver half dollar on the counter. It skidded and went on the floor, but Shelby made no move to pick it up. The storekeeper recovered it and turned it over and over in his fingers. "Don't see much silver no more."

Shelby wrote his note, folded it, put it in the envelope, and sealed it. He addressed the envelope to "Señor Andrés Díaz, San Antonio, Texas," and handed it to the storekeeper. "Will you take care of this?"

"Yes, sir. Be glad to." He glanced at Shelby's horse outside. "Do ye know where a man could buy anything he could sell at a profit, these days?"

Shelby shook his head, his lower lip loose. "I'm not a merchant, myself."

"Well, just thought I'd ask."

Shelby went out and got on his horse. He didn't

want to take a chance on meeting somebody who might know him. He rode ten miles before he stopped to camp. He built a small fire and made some coffee. He ate some *carne colorada* dry, and washed it down with the coffee. Then he unbridled the horse and took off the saddle. He staked out the horse, rolled up in his blanket, and went to sleep.

At mid-afternoon the next day he rode into a chaparral thicket, looked at the cloudless sky, and howled like a coyote before a storm. In a few minutes a whiskered man appeared, holding his rifle ahead of him.

"All right, Shelby," he said, pointing with the rifle. "This way. I'll go first. The camp is moved again."

"Who's bothering you?" asked Shelby, following.

"That damn Confederate captain keeps ridin' out here."

Shelby said scornfully, "He's looking for conscripts."

"He might decide *we* look like conscripts."

"I don't think so. The Confederates have got their hands full as it is."

They crossed an open space, skirted a mud bog, and went through a thick clump of mesquite that was taller than a man on a horse. The smell of burning cedar drifted through the brush, and then they broke into a small clearing. The mesquite around was littered with garments and hung with canteens, and here and there a rifle leaned against a bush. Joe Cooper sat with his back against a saddle, the muscles of his heavy face loosened by the whisky that was undoubtedly missing from the keg between his knees.

"S'down," he said, "and wet your whistle."

Shelby helped himself to a drink. He was right: the jug was almost empty.

"What's the job you got for me now?" asked Cooper.

Shelby sat down, one hand on the jug. "I want you and Jesús to ride over to Turtle Creek, in Kerr County. Tegener will be there with fifty or a hundred men. You watch them but stay out of sight. Bergmann will tell you if there is any change of plans."

"How long you want me to stay?"

Shelby's vocal sibilance was more pronounced with the whisky inside of him. He had another drink. "Stay until Duff catches them."

"What happens when they get to the border?"

"It will happen *before* they get to the border. Now just do what I say." He had another drink. "Duff will pay you."

The liquor was warm in his empty stomach. It went all through him and relaxed him. His eyes got blurry but he kept drinking, until presently he fell over on top of the jug.

Cooper reached out with one big arm and pushed him away from the jug. Shelby's head, loose on his shoulders, bumped on the soft turf, and he lay still, snoring. Cooper recovered the jug and drained it. Then he called hoarsely, "Ned!"

Ned Hungerford appeared. Cooper's head rolled from side to side, his eyes loose in their sockets. "Search him!" he ordered.

Ned found two double-gooses. "Gold!" he said. "Ain't seen that much in weeks."

"Nev' mind. Put it—in my shirt."

"He'll know you got it when he wakes up."

"He won't know nothin'," said Cooper. "He never remembers nothin' that happens when he's drinkin'. Why else do you think I'd let him soak up my whisky?"

Shelby rolled a little and said without opening his eyes, "One thing more, Cooper."

"What is it?"

"Be back here by the twentieth. They're going to get the quinine in Monterrey the twenty-fourth. An' another thing."

"I'm listenin'," Cooper growled.

"Don't take the gold. Just see they get it safe to Monterrey."

"Whatsamatter with gold?" asked Cooper.

"Nothing—but quinine's worth more. Wait for the quinine."

Cooper looked at Ned. "He's crazy," he growled. "Nothin's worth more than gold."

"Don't argue," said Shelby, his eyes still closed. "Do what I said." Then he began to snore.

CHAPTER XVIII

BUASS HALL was packed before sundown. General Houston was in town; nobody knew exactly where, but the fact of his presence in Austin was enough to insure interest—and most likely fireworks.

Talley found a place to stand against the wall at one side. Garrison and Shelby were on the platform, along with Scarbrough and former Governor Clark. Houston was nowhere in sight. Garrison seemed to be watching the door for a signal. Suddenly he stepped up to the speakers' table and addressed the crowd:

"Ladies and gentlemen, we are privileged tonight to hear from a man whose word has been law in Texas for thirty years. Tennessee and Virginia have produced many great men, but none like Sam Houston."

Somebody in the middle of the hall made a derisive noise, but Garrison went on:

"Ladies and gentlemen, it is my privilege to introduce that great man—former governor of two states, former United States senator, former president of the Texas Republic—General Sam Houston!"

The great frame of Sam Houston appeared. He was nearly seventy years old but still six-feet-two or -three—some said six-feet-six, and indeed it was easy to believe—and still straight as the proverbial Indian arrow, still square-shouldered. He stood in the doorway for a moment, and such was the power of his personality that he seemed to be looking at each person present. He advanced up the aisle in long strides, his Indian moccasins crunching softly on the board floor. He reached the platform, shook hands with Garrison and Clark and Scarbrough, but ignored Shelby. Then he turned and faced the audience.

His blue eyes were deep-set and penetrating, his brows heavy and thunderous, his forehead high, his hair white, and he spoke in a bass voice that seemed to reverberate all through the building.

"Some of you," he said, "have laughed to scorn the idea of bloodshed resulting from secession, and I have heard men in this very hall say jestingly that they would drink all the blood that would flow in consequence of it! The time may come when that will appear to have been a prophetic statement. The time will come when your fathers and husbands, your sons and brothers, will be herded together like sheep and cattle at the point of the bayonet.

"The South might, after the sacrifice of millions of dollars and hundreds of thousands of lives, win independence, if God be not against you; but I doubt it. I believe in the doctrine of states' rights, but I tell you the North is determined to preserve this union. They are not an impulsive people as you are, but when they begin to move in a given direction they move with the steady momentum and perseverance of an avalanche, and I fear they will overwhelm the South with defeat.

"Secession is not a subject to be determined. You have already voted for it, and now the real question is whether you shall divide into factions and fight among yourselves. That would be a still greater calamity. What has happened has happened, and you must not fight among yourselves. But I tell you this: your rivers will run red with the blood of the best citizens of Texas; the bat and the owl will take up their abode in your houses, and the grass will grow green in your streets."

The crowd had sobered. The magnetism of Sam Houston's voice and the tremendous power of his presence quieted them. Houston talked on—not as long as Talley had previously heard him, for he seemed obviously tired. Then presently—too soon, almost—he had finished talking, shook hands again with all but Shelby, and was going back down the aisle.

Talley tried to figure out what he had said. It seemed to be yes on one hand and no on the other, and Talley could not see that they were any closer to an answer. There was no denying that Houston had been essentially right, but Talley felt that even Houston no longer knew a solution, and for a moment it was a weakening thought. Sam Houston had always been the great man of Texas, and it had been in the back of every man's mind that, no matter what trouble the state might get into, Sam Houston would come forth and tell them what to do and help them do it. And now Talley—and perhaps others—was facing the harsh truth that they were in a mess and that even General Houston was without power to pull them out of it.

Houston was at the door when B. B. Davis jumped up and shouted, "Let's hang the damned old scoundrel!" He started to lunge down the aisle, but somebody stuck out a foot and Davis fell head over heels. Houston waited, his majestic mien unshaken. Davis got up, his impulsive determination wilted, his poise gone. Houston looked at him scathingly.

"Be seated, ladies, be seated. The feists always bark at the big dog." He turned and left.

Garrison began to talk again. "You heard the words of General Houston," he said. "Is there any man here who would not listen to the man who whipped Santa Anna?"

Somebody in the back apparently saw it the same as Talley, for he heard a murmured, "What did Houston say anyway?"

Garrison was going on: "A company of innocent men, men who want nothing but peace and quiet, are now headed for Mexico—but Captain Duff has been ordered to stop them. How much more violation of human rights do we have to

198

endure from these monsters who sit in Richmond?"

"Them's strong words, Reverend," said Frank Ballard.

"I've told the truth," said Garrison. "Is anybody here afraid of the truth?"

Ballard asked wisely, "Is there anybody that ain't?"

Paul Scarbrough came to his feet, "Reverend," he said, "I don't want to be disrespectful, but ranting isn't going to do any good."

Garrison began to redden. He looked over the audience. "You, Abraham Tilden!" he shouted. "You had two sons conscripted. What are you going to do about it?"

Tilden tried to speak but couldn't find his voice. He cleared his throat and tried again. "There ain't much you can do," he said finally, "when they say they want you."

Now old Eph Dunstan, filled with corn whisky—as were a good many of them, to judge from the smell in the room—swayed to his feet. "We'll hang Jeff Davis to a sour apple tree!" he chanted.

Talley saw Dujet slide out the door. The Creole might be hotheaded but he was no fool.

Shelby was on his feet, shouting at Garrison. The Reverend, red-faced, pushed Shelby to avoid falling off the platform. Ned Hungerford and an older man appeared and laid hands on the

Reverend. Women screamed. Half a dozen more laid hands on Hungerford and his sidekick. Paul Scarbrough got in between Garrison and Shelby. He was only trying to separate them, but Garrison stumbled and fell, and a wave of shouting men flowed over Scarbrough.

"Hang 'im, hang 'im, hang 'im!" shouted Jud Montague, standing on a chair.

The speakers' table went over, and Moore swung a chair at the kerosene lamp above it. The glass globe exploded, leaving a trail of burning oil, and those below it surged toward the door.

Talley tried to get to the corner to put out the fire, but the spectators who had been in that corner were frenziedly fighting their way to the exit. The oil on the floor burned bright yellow and gave off clouds of black smoke, and flames began to eat into the dry wood.

A general fight was raging over and around the platform. The ladies on the far side were moving toward the door, headed by Adele. At that moment B. B. Davis appeared from somewhere with a stuffed scarecrow. Undoubtedly it had been prearranged, and Davis met the first refugees from the burning corner and shouted, "Let's hang 'im!"

The fleeing men slowed down.

"Hang 'im!" shouted a dozen voices.

The scarecrow, stuffed with straw, had a high

silk hat fastened to the top and an old black Prince Albert coat around its middle.

"Hang Jeff Davis!" shouted Mumpy Moore.

It might have been that the effigy of Jefferson Davis saved them from a tragedy, for B. B. Davis, Eph and Jud and Mumpy Moore turned around and led the way out of the hall, with the audience falling in behind them, and the hall was emptied in two or three minutes.

Mumpy Moore was carrying a lantern. They led the crowd to a big oak tree. Eph produced a rope which they tied around the effigy's neck, and Jud drenched it with kerosene from a lamp snatched from the hall. They threw the other end of the rope over a limb, and somebody struck a match. The straw stuffing blazed, and at every twitch of the rope, burning straw fell to the ground, and men shouted and cheered.

Talley looked back. Buass Hall was burning fiercely. The shingles had gone and some of the siding, but the scantlings that formed the roof were like black diagonals drenched with flame.

Jud shouted, "Scarbrough! Where's Paul Scarbrough? He started it!"

"He's run home to hide!" said Frank Ballard, also infected with the fever.

"Let's go git 'im!" said Davis.

Twenty or more men started toward Paul Scarbrough's house, about a block away, and Talley, now considerably worried, went along.

Scarbrough, however, had seen what might come of this, and there was nobody home. He had gotten his wife and three children out and gone somewhere else. But B. B. Davis was on a rampage.

"Burn the house!" he shouted. Somebody threw kerosene on it, and a moment later it also was going up in flames.

Talley looked around for Garrison but couldn't locate him. Maybe at last the Reverend had realized what a monster he had created by his constant haranguing and had thought it best to retreat from the scene of violence.

Eph shouted above the crackling flames, "Hey, Shelby, you out here reportin' for the *Bugle*?"

Shelby's face, in the light of the burning house, suddenly showed alarm. "I'm just lookin' on," he said.

But there was already a crowd around him. "You'll have to report who did it, won't you?"

Shelby began to back away. "I don't know who did it," he said.

Eph Dunstan said loudly, "Maybe we ought to give him some of the same, boys."

Shelby cursed him and began to run. He was pursued, but in a few seconds he had lost them in the dark.

"Let's get the printing office!" somebody shouted.

This could go on forever, apparently—or at

least until the town of Austin was in ashes. Talley cupped his hands to his mouth and shouted, "Troops! Troops! Run for your lives!"

The mob spirit sagged for a moment. Talley started running toward his horse. He reached the *bayo,* looked back, and saw the men milling, not quite knowing what to do. He pulled the rifle out of its boot and fired two shots in the air. "Troops!" he shouted, and fired three times more.

He swung into the saddle and turned the *bayo* toward the northwest at a hard gallop. That did it. Before he was shut off from sight of the mob around Scarbrough's house he looked back and saw no man anywhere. With luck there would be no more burnings that night.

Talley went home from the burning in effigy of Jefferson Davis with considerable uneasiness. He could understand well enough the impatience of men who had not favored the war anyway—for even the seccession ordinance had been defeated in Travis County by a 4-to-1 vote—but he was alarmed at the violence of feeling he had seen that night. When Robertson heard about it, there could very well be military law again in Travis County.

It was midnight when he turned up the long slope, and he was astonished to see a light still in the window.

He put the saddle and bridle in the shed, where it would be protected from rain, and turned the *bayo* into the meadow. He went down to the water and washed his hands and face. Then he went back to the cabin. Through the window, he saw his mother sitting in the rawhide chair. She had a shawl close about her shoulders. He opened the door and went in.

His mother's eyes were dull. Though wrapped tightly in two blankets, she shivered violently as he approached her.

"I been afraid of this," his mother said. "The miasms are thick at night."

Talley was thoughtful. "There's been lots of pools lately, now that the river has gone down."

"I had a fire tonight to purify the air—but it didn't help."

He laid his hand on her forearm. "Had the fever yet?"

"Not yet."

"I better get back to Austin and see the doctor. He'll have some medicine." He touched her hand. It was cold—so cold it almost scared him. He said, "Don't worry. I'll get the doctor."

The moon was getting low when he reached town. He let the *bayo* down to a walk, turned left at the hotel and went three blocks, past the great pile of hot embers that marked the site of Buass Hall.

The doctor's house was dark, but Talley did not see a buggy in the shed. He got down and knocked on the door.

After a little he heard movement on the bare floor. Then a lamp was lighted, and the doctor's wife, in a long white nightgown and a knitted wrapper, came to the door, opened it, and looked out. "Who's there?" she asked.

Talley stepped into the light. "It's none of my business, ma'am," he said, touching his hatbrim, "but the way things are these days you shouldn't open your door until you know who is on the other side."

"Oh, pshaw, Roy Talley. Nobody is going to bother me. The door isn't locked anyway. Now what's the matter? Your ma sick?"

"She's got the chills."

"I doubt there's anything he can do, but you're welcome to ask him."

"Where is he now?"

"Eph's wife is havin' a baby." She snorted. "Lazy good-for-nothin'. Too bad he can't be put to work. That's nine babies in eleven years."

"Thank you, ma'am. I'll go talk to him."

He found Eph's house on the edge of town. There were candles burning in two rooms, and he knocked.

"Come in!" Eph was sitting in a rawhide-bottom chair with a jug of whisky on the floor beside him, and Talley guessed the jug was mighty near empty. Through the open doorway he saw Eph's wife, her wind-tanned face white as the labor pain struck her, gripping the iron posts of the bedstead over her head. The oldest girl, about ten, was holding the baby in one arm while she fed wood into the stove to heat a dishpan full of water. Dr. Kenedy, broad-shouldered and heavy-framed, with thick gray whiskers down the sides of his face, looked sourly at him through smeary glasses.

"What's going on at *your* place?" he growled.

"Ma's got the chills."

The doctor had rolled up his sleeves and tucked his vest into his pants. "She had 'em before. Prob'ly comin' back on her. Maybe it won't be too bad."

"I thought I'd better see you."

The doctor glanced at Eph's wife and then at Eph. "Not much I can do, Roy, even if I wasn't busy."

"You could give us some medicine, maybe."

"Quinine?" The doctor said sourly, "Not a pill in Austin." He shook his head resignedly as Eph's wife groaned again. "If the Union don't lick us, the chills will do the job."

"Haven't you got a few pills in your case?"

"Not a pill!" He said to the girl, "Sary, that water about ready?"

She looked up, a wild-appearing little thing with great blue eyes almost hidden by disheveled cotton-colored hair. She stuck the tip of one finger into the dishpan. "It's warm," she said.

The doctor watched Eph's wife for a moment,

gauging her pains. "Warm or hot, it'll have to do. It looks like your ma's time is just about to come."

Talley said, "You need any help?"

Kenedy shook his head. "Not for her. She delivers easy. But I'll tell you what to do with your ma."

"Yes."

The doctor got a pair of scissors out of his case. "Keep her wrapped up when she has the chills. Give her hot drinks—whisky if you've got it."

Roy nodded.

"When she has fever," said the doctor, pointing with his scissors, "give her cold drinks—tamarind water, cream of tartar water with sugar, if you've got it, flavored with orange. Be careful she doesn't have a chill when she's sweating." He turned to glower at Talley. "Now either roll up your sleeves or get out of my way."

It was daylight when Talley returned to the ranch. His mother was napping in the chair, but she woke up at his touch on the door. He told her what the doctor had said. It troubled her when he told her there was no quinine.

"I never treated chills without quinine," she said.

"It isn't to be had, Ma. We'll have to do the best we can."

He put his arm across her shoulders. "You'll get along," he assured her. "I'll lay down for a while."

"Take a cup of hot coffee. I'll call if I need you."

He nodded, took the cup, and lay down on the bed. It was fine to get out of his boots, and he was asleep in a few minutes.

CHAPTER XIX

HE WOKE UP to the sound of pounding hoofs. He swung his feet to the floor and slid into his boots almost before he got his eyes open. B. B. Davis, knees flying, loped up on a horse as gaunt and awkward as he was. Talley went out to meet him.

"You know them men with Major Tegener?" Davis asked.

"Yes."

"The word is they are headin' for Mexico—but they are headin' for a trap laid by Captain Duff."

Talley looked at him. "How do you know?"

"Your brothers are with 'em, and Cap'n Robertson thought you might like to know."

"Robertson?" Talley thought for a moment. That meant only one thing: Robertson was suggesting he try to warn Tegener. He pushed his hat back and looked toward the other cabin. "Don't tell Ma about the boys," he said.

Davis's eyes widened. "I better get on back."

When Mrs. Talley came to the door Davis had gone. "Roy," she said, "what are you getting into now?"

He answered seriously. "I don't know, Ma. Maybe nothing."

"There are enough of us in trouble," she said.

"Ma," he asked sharply, "how did you know anybody's in trouble?"

"If somebody wasn't, Davis wouldn't have come after you."

"I'll be careful," he said.

"You've always been one I could count on." Her voice was a little wistful. "You're hard-headed and independent as a hog on ice, but you've always been levelheaded. I hope you stay that way."

"I'll try, Ma. You stay inside and keep warm."

He saddled up and rode off. His mother was standing in the yard, shading her eyes with her hand, and he had a glimpse of the feelings she kept inside of her. On an impulse he did something he hadn't done in years: he waved at her. Then he trotted off down the river.

It was still daylight in Austin when Talley tied the *bayo* in front of the millinery shop and went to the door.

Mrs. Partridge's voice sounded from the back room. "Come in."

He opened the door. She was standing by the window and now she turned. "Sit down, Roy. I'll make some tea."

"I haven't time for that, ma'am." He pushed his

hat back on his head. "But I thought this would be a good time to settle our plans."

"The twelfth is Tuesday," she said.

"Have you spoken to Moore about a horse?"

"Yes, he promised me a good saddle horse."

"We'll have to go down through Edinburg and Reynosa," he said. "There is too much trouble higher up on the river."

"Aren't there guards?"

"I know the Rio Grande down there, ma'am. We won't have any trouble on that score." He went on, "There's a full moon tonight, and it will rise about 8:30 on Tuesday night. We'll get started at sundown, as I said before."

"But you will head for Beeville first?"

He hesitated a moment before he answered, "Yes." He knew now it had been a good hunch to tell her the route—which he did not intend to follow. He wondered whom she would relay it to.

"And we'll come back the same way?"

"Probably. Now I've got to go."

There was a knock at the door. She looked up and said, "Come in." Captain Robertson stepped inside.

"Do you know anything about that mob down there, Talley?"

"Not too much," said Talley. "I understand they're riled up on account of Duff forcing a battle with Tegener."

Robertson looked worried. "If you have any influence with them, you'd better send them home. If a large group of men like that starts riding across country, anything can happen."

"Such as what?"

Robertson frowned. "A man riding cross-country with a rifle in his boot might be considered physically able to fight."

"Sounds reasonable."

"Public meetings are one thing, but burning in effigy is something else, and now an armed mob with the avowed purpose of seeking battle with Confederate forces—can you do anything to stop it?"

"I don't know—but I'll tell you one thing, Captain: everybody in the country knows that Tegener was heading for the border peacefully. If Duff sheds blood, it will be on his own head."

"It is not as simple as that, Mr. Talley." Robertson half arose. "This is serious. Lives will be lost if somebody doesn't make them understand."

Talley got up. "I'll do what I can." He nodded at Helen Partridge. "I'll see you, ma'am."

He went slowly toward the post office, where most of the crowd seemed to be. Somehow or other Mrs. Partridge was too smooth. Was that just her way, or was it something else? It would be hard to know.

He went into the post office and talked to

George Hancock, Moore, Giles, and a dozen others. It was noticeable that there was no representative there from Governor Lubbock's office.

"There's one thing about it," Talley told them. "It's a hundred-and-fifty-mile ride to the Nueces. That's two good days. You couldn't get there in time, so you might as well wait for more news. Maybe it won't be as bad as it looks."

"I got no confidence in them Confederate troops," said Moore, "but you're right about not being able to get there in time to help. It's strange nobody thought of that."

He walked with Moore to the livery, leading the *bayo*. "I got to make a hurry trip to San Antone. You got a saddle horse that can spell the *bayo?*"

Moore looked a little dubious, but he said, "I got a couple of good horses. You can take your pick."

He took the coyote dun—one with a black stripe down its back. It had mustang blood and would keep going until it dropped. He said to Moore, "Be back in three or four days."

He alternated horses and hit San Antonio the next night. He took the horses to Los Caballos for feeding, and got a few hours' sleep in the loft above them. He was on the road at sunup. Toward late afternoon he pulled in at a blacksmith shop on the outskirts of the town of Uvalde. The smith looked up from his forge.

"I'm Talley—Roy Talley."

"I've heard of you." He looked at the horses. "You don't need any shoes on them animals."

Talley leaned over. "I want to find Tegener and his men."

"I don't know nothin' about it." The smith began to hammer a strip of iron.

"Duff is after them," Talley said.

The smith studied him. "I can tell you where to find them," he said, "but if you're a Confederate spy I'll twist your neck."

"I'm not. I've got two brothers with them."

The smith nodded. "Follow the road west to Del Rio. They're camped along the river there."

He reached the camp before sundown, and Tom was one of the first to meet him. Tom's eyes narrowed and he asked belligerently, "What are you doin' down here? Come to tell us what we can do again?"

"I want to see Major Tegener."

Tom sneered and waved at the scattered camp. "Help yourself. He's up there somewhere."

The major's tent was pitched in a thin cedar brake a couple of hundred yards west of the river. Talley rode up to the fire where Tegener and Bergmann were cooking strips of deer meat suspended from pointed sticks.

"Get down, Talley," said Tegener. "You going with us?"

Talley alighted and dropped the reins of the

213

bayo. "Major, I came to warn you again. Duff has been sent after you."

The major leaned back and shook his head. He was a big, well-built man. "No," he said, "Duff wouldn't come after us. We're not harming anything."

Talley accepted a cup of coffee from Bergmann. "Duff is out to make a name for himself," he insisted.

"Then why didn't he do it in Kerr County?"

"Maybe he didn't have orders."

Tegener brushed it aside with a wave of his hand. "They won't bother us. We aren't doing anything."

CHAPTER XX

BUT MANY THINGS had been happening, and only some of them were known to Tegener. A man named John Sansom had joined the Tegener party on Turtle Creek. At that time there had been eighty men, but the following day, when the party started for Mexico, only sixty-one set out under Major Tegener. Among these were Sansom, Tom and Jim Talley, and the traitor Bergmann, whose job was to keep the Confederate officials informed of the whereabouts and plans of the Tegener party.

For eight days they had proceeded leisurely to the Nueces. Tegener insisted that they were doing nothing wrong and therefore could not be injured; likewise, although he knew that Confederate troops were hunting them, he believed they had evaded them, and the entire affair became a sort of vacation, with men hunting, playing games, and in general enjoying the trip.

On the eighth day, four more men joined them, and on the morning of the next day they crossed the Nueces River and pitched camp two hundred yards west of the river in a comparatively open brake of cedar trees. Two men were assigned as horse guards. Deer, turkeys and javelinas were plentiful along the river, and the entire command split up into hunting parties, with fun as important an object as meat.

In the meantime, Lieut. C. D. McRae had been sent out from San Antonio to break up the company. With him were ninety-four men, including a detachment from Captain Donalson's Company, one from Captain Davis's Company, and one from Taylor's Battalion. Under him also was a detachment of Duff's Partisan Rangers, and McRae depended heavily on the advice of Duff, who, though known to be severe, nevertheless was relied upon because of his demonstrated ability to bring order in unruly communities.

McRae's men, well-armed with new repeating rifles, and kept informed by Bergmann, drew close as the men hunted and amused themselves all of that ninth day. At a council of his staff, McRae made plans to assemble two striking forces in cedar brakes within attacking distance of Tegener's camp, and to attack by daylight the next morning. Duff and his proved campaigners were to lead the attack.

"Aye, and we'll make a lesson of them all," said Duff.

McRae asked, "Do you think we should kill them?"

"What else?" asked Duff. "This is war, and they'll be fighting with rifles and pistols. It's hardly to be expected that we can conquer them with nigger-shooters."

McRae nodded. "The main thing is, they need to be taught a lesson. The state of Texas will never support the Confederacy as long as men are allowed to come and go as they please."

Duff nodded. "I know some of the men in Tegener's party. There are a couple of Talley boys with them—and a more unruly pair never set out for Mexico."

Donalson said, "It is a hardheaded family."

Duff's blue eyes were smoldering as he answered. "Their mother held a rifle on me and ordered me off the ranch. People like that must learn their lesson."

McRae seemed a little uneasy, but he ended the council. "Duff, take your men into concealment in one of these brakes. The other party will flank them, and I think between us we will have no trouble."

"It's going to be touch-and-go," said Donalson, "moving into position during the day. Tegener's men are roaming over the countryside like children. We may be seen."

McRae snorted. "Tegener's a fool. He thinks he has given us the slip. We'll move into position by dark."

At about sunset, soon after Talley arrived, one of the Tegener hunting parties galloped back to the major's tent and breathlessly informed him that they had seen a number of armed men slipping through the brush along the bank of the river. Tegener at first was alarmed, and his feeling spread throughout the camp. Men gathered near his tent, seeing to their rifles, but many of these were only muzzle-loaders, and one or two Mexicans had no weapons at all.

Tegener was about to send out a scouting party when another group of hunters came in and listened for a few minutes in amusement, then announced that they were the strangers; that they had allowed themselves to be seen and then had hidden, so as to frighten the first party.

This explanation suited Tegener. He laughed and said it was a good joke. The members of the first party were raw-hided for being missionaries or greenhorns, and then a third party came in and verified the entire story.

Tegener sent men out to catch and stake the horses, and detailed a night guard. And they were still teasing the men who had seen the supposed strangers when they began a sumptuous supper on the game that had been brought in.

It was during the relaxation following the meal, after the men had taken their tin plates and cups down to the river for washing, that it came out that the third party had seen strangers not toward the east or southeast, but in a cedar brake directly south of the Tegener camp.

Roy Talley and some others were alarmed, but Major Tegener and Captain Kuechler and Lieutenant Degener, a young man who had joined them at Turtle Creek, passed it off. If there were any such strangers around, they said, they would have made themselves known, for there was no need for secrecy. Some of the men—especially the few older ones—felt uneasy, but the officers reassured them.

After supper the younger men turned to games—leapfrog, wrestling, somersault contests, jumping, knife throwing. And over it all Tegener presided like a wise and indulgent father, feeling very expansive as he watched these men enjoying themselves. "Look out over this group, Mr. Talley," he said. "Have you ever seen a more childlike, fun-loving camp of men in your life? It is entirely innocent fun. Nobody could accuse us of any intention even of breaking the peace."

Talley looked off into the distance. It was odd there were no coyotes singing that night. "I am trying to look at it from the viewpoint of a professional soldier who has been ordered to put an end to migration to Mexico," he said. "He would not be interested in your peaceful intentions, but only in the fact that you are conducting to Mexico a large number of men who are physically qualified to serve in the Confederate army."

Tegener seemed amused. "You have said that before, Mr. Talley." He sipped his coffee. "You will note the fires are dying down and the young men are tiring of their games. We will have speeches now, and then to a restful sleep."

The men gathered around Tegener's fire, some sitting close, some in the shadows with their backs against the trees. Kuechler made a talk in his broken English on "The Fatherland." Captain Kramer spoke in German on "Citizenship." Others talked on "The Civil War" and "Migrating to Mexico."

Roy Talley and John Sansom, being both uneasy, had made a slow round of the camp just beyond the cedars. The night was quiet and peaceful; the stars were brilliant, and there was only the occasional stamp of horses who would soon be settling down for their short before-midnight sleep.

"The very peacefulness," said John Sansom, "is like a premonition."

"You're right," Talley agreed. "It's *too* quiet."

"Do you think as I do, that the Confederates are dangerous?"

"I have seen Duff." He paused. "He understands a rifle pointed at his stomach, but little else."

They went back to Tegener's tent, and Sansom called him away from the fire. "Major," he said, "I am not satisfied that the two hunting parties saw another hunting party. I think they saw Confederate troops laying an ambush for us."

Tegener wagged his head from side to side. "Oh, *ja,* some people imagine a fight very easily."

Talley spoke up. "Do you realize, Major, that the two spots mentioned by your parties—one on the east and one on the south—would have your camp flanked perfectly?"

Tegener shook his head. "You are both assuming they want to fight a battle—but we have no intention of fighting."

Talley looked at Sansom. Sansom said, "Major, let us do guard duty tonight."

"There's no need of either of you doing guard duty. The guard has been sent out."

Sansom said, "Will you have the guard call me at two o'clock?"

"*Ja,* sure. Anything to settle your mind."

Talley said, "Major, the moon is bright and the night air would make cool traveling. Why don't you break camp and start for Mexico? You could cross the Rio Grande in one march—and then your entire command would be safe."

Tegener moistened his lips thoughtfully, and Sansom threw in his arguments. Tegener began to think seriously. "I will call the officers," he said, "and see if they feel we should move on."

Captain Kuechler, Captain Kramer, Lieutenant Degener and Lieutenant Simon gathered, and Tegener put the question to them. "These two men—Sansom and Talley—are nervous about the possibility of attack by the Confederates. They suggest that we break camp and head for the Rio Grande at once."

"Now?" exclaimed Kuechler.

"Yes, tonight."

"The moon is shining," said Kramer. "It would not be difficult."

"You can be under way in half an hour," Sansom urged.

"Major," said Lieutenant Degener, "I was with the party to the south, and I don't think they saw Confederate troops. There were no uniforms and no military equipment."

"The troops in Texas don't have many uniforms," Talley pointed out, "and most of them provide their own equipment."

"Nevertheless," said Kuechler, "I have to agree that the so-called strangers were really men of our own party. I see no use," he continued, "of alarming our men with this continued talk of enemy attack. I think the best thing is to get a good night's sleep and continue our march tomorrow. I doubt very much that the Confederates are within fifty miles of us."

Talley insisted, "If they are, you're taking a chance. Duff goes after Unionists like a badger after a rabbit."

"Well, gentlemen," said Tegener, still unperturbed, "I think it best we retire." He smiled. "You see, Mr. Talley, you cannot work up much enthusiasm for your warlike ideas."

Talley and Sansom lay down near each other, both fully dressed and with loaded rifles at their sides. Talley awoke as a hand touched his shoulder and his name was called quietly at the same time. "Want to take a look around?"

Talley sat up and began to pull on his boots. "What time is it?"

"Nearly three. The guard, Bauer, is about to take a turn down to the cedar brake on the east. We'll follow him."

Bauer went quietly, a shadowy ghost in the predawn darkness. Talley and Sansom stayed twenty feet behind. Talley was walking on the balls of his feet, his rifle across his chest. They drew closer to the cedar brake which, unlike Tegener's, was dense with underbrush. Bauer had just gone into the brake when a red-and-yellow flash lit up the area and the dull boom of a black-powder explosion temporarily deafened them. Sansom, his rifle in position, fired back, and then suddenly the brake was alive with Confederate soldiers.

The Confederates fired a few shots, but sixty or more of them—obviously awakened by the shots—swarmed out of the brake and retreated across open ground to another part of the grove some sixty yards away.

In the dark, Talley turned Bauer's body over and felt his temple. He looked at the small hole left of his breastbone; he turned him over and felt his back, wet with blood. "He's dead."

"I hit their guard," Sansom said, "but he got away."

Firing had started from the farther brake, and Talley and Sansom ran back. Firing was also coming from the Unionist camp, and a man fell just ahead of them.

"Ernest Bosler, the other guard!" shouted Sansom.

Talley bent low. Bosler too was dead.

But now they had to reach the shelter of the Tegener camp, for the Confederates, with wild yells, were starting a charge on foot from the farther brake. Some of them were hit by Unionist bullets, but they came on, only to break at the edge of the cedars. The Unionists, urged by Kuechler, made a countercharge but did not follow very far, for the muzzle-loaders were good for only one shot and then required reloading by hand.

Talley and Sansom found Tegener bleeding plentifully from three wounds. He was lying on his pallet with his rifle barrel over his saddle, waiting for the enemy. Captain Kramer and Lieutenant Simon had been wounded.

"There are close to a hundred Confederate troops out there!" Sansom told Tegener. "You must withdraw at once!"

"It's too open in here," said Talley. "You have no cover. They can spot you from two hundred yards away."

Tegener looked up. His mouth hung loosely, and he was obviously in pain. "It might be best," he conceded.

But four men, including a Mexican named Pablo Díaz who had nothing but a very rusty old flintlock, wanted to stay and fight.

Sansom and Talley went to find the other officers and propose moving. Sansom found Degener near the edge of the brake. Degener, watching for a renewal of the Confederate attack, asked about Tegener's plans.

"He has about decided to withdraw to a better position."

"Withdraw!" Degener exclaimed. "Not me! We'll lose all our baggage and our horses if we leave, and my men would rather fight until they are killed. We were here peaceably, and the attack was unprovoked. No, sir." He shook his head stubbornly. "We'll fight until every man is dead."

Sansom said earnestly, "Hugo, we're heavily outnumbered and we're holding a very poor position. As for horses, we might very well get some of theirs in the excitement."

But Degener would not hear of it, and Talley moved around until he found Tom and Jim. "You boys better come with me," he said.

"What for?" asked Tom.

"Because we can't defend this place. We've got to leave."

Tom asked sullenly, "What does the major say?"

"I don't know yet."

"If he wants to stay and fight, we'll stay and fight," Tom said.

Talley shook his head. "It will be slaughter. They've got twice as many men, and they're all armed and all fighting men. They've got us flanked on two sides."

"I ain't running," said Tom.

"How about you, Jim?"

"I'll stay with Tom. We can handle our own affairs."

Talley downed the great impatience that was building up in him. "Have you both got rifles and pistols?"

"We're armed," said Tom.

"I ought to give you both a gun-whipping and take you home."

"You ain't big enough," said Tom.

"I'm big enough to whip you, but I couldn't drag you out of here."

"First time I ever heard you admit there was something you couldn't do," said Tom.

Talley shook his head sadly. "You're playing at kid stuff," he said. "This is no game. The Confederates will come to kill you when it's daylight."

"Then you run," said Tom. "We'll stay and fight."

Talley went back to Tegener's tent, grim but helpless.

Sansom said, "There's three will go with us. We'll carry our saddles and start for the horses."

It was now almost dawn. Sansom and Talley, with three others, left Tegener's camp and hid in the brush along the river about halfway between the two camps.

When the first gray broke in the east, the Confederates poured out of their two camps, yelling and shooting. They were met with heavy fire from Tegener's camp. Apparently the officers were directing the men to fire alternately so they could not be caught with empty rifles, for the fire was fairly steady. Talley and Sansom and their comrades, from their hiding places in the brush, fired at the Confederates from the flank, but the range was long.

The Confederates charged again to the edge of the brake but were driven back by steady fire.

Then Duff strode fearlessly behind the ragged line, cursing and threatening and urging the men to charge. He was identifiable by his big, square frame and his sandy hair.

The Confederates renewed the attack and charged to the edge of the cedar brake and into it. The Unionist fire was dying. Talley saw Tegener and a small group of Unionists run from the brake on the northwest, toward the horse herd. He watched for Tom and Jim, but could not make them out.

"Those who can walk are leaving," Sansom said in a low voice. "The wounded have to stay behind."

"Yes," said Talley. "I wonder what Duff will do with those who are left."

"Bandage up their wounds and take them to San Antone and put them in the army."

Talley looked at him. "I'm going to stay around and see."

"We don't dare stay long," Sansom said. "Our horses will give us away."

"We're a long way from their camp. We'd have a good head start."

Sansom shook his head. "You've got two brothers up there, haven't you?"

"Yes."

"I know how you feel," said Sansom, "but remember something: McRae's outfit is not the only one in the country. They've been hunting

Unionists for weeks, and they've probably got other parties out along the Nueces. We *could* get caught between two fires."

Talley considered, and finally nodded. "You take the others and go. I'll unsaddle my horse and stake it out in those oak trees. I'm going to stay long enough to find out what happens."

Sansom caught up his bridle. "Good luck."

Talley nodded. He was still watching the camp, and he would have given a good deal for a pair of field glasses.

Within a few minutes he was startled to see Tom, hatless, run with a hoarse scream into the open. Duff appeared behind him with a rifle. The rifle boomed, and Tom leaped forward, his arms outstretched, and skidded along the grass on his face. At the end of his forward movement, he lay still.

Now Jim Talley staggered to his feet and advanced on Duff, his mouth cursing.

Duff glanced at him, then sidestepped and tripped him. Jim fell on his back and Talley, watching, gasped and sighted along his rifle. But it was too far.

Jim Talley, with his hands and feet tied, was pushed under a big oak tree on the west edge of the cedar brake. A sergeant flung the loose end of the rope over a limb, and set a hangman's knot under his left jaw. An officer barked, "Detail! Take the rope!"

And at that moment Jim Talley did something he had not done for many years. He burst out sobbing. Talley shouted hoarsely, but he was across the river and they didn't even hear him.

Duff raised his hand. The four-man detail backed away and took up the slack, and left Jim Talley standing there, a slim, gangly boy of sixteen, hardly able to stay on his feet, sobbing in utter frustration.

Duff's arm dropped. The detail hauled hard on the rope, and Jim's sobbing stopped abruptly. His body swung in the air, and his struggles stopped in a moment or two.

Duff went back into the brake, and there were pistol shots and hoarse cries. They were killing the wounded.

CHAPTER XXI

WITH HATRED building up in every bone in his body, Talley went slowly down to where the *bayo* was tied. With half a dozen men he would have charged the Confederate camp—but he was alone.

He looked back once—at Jim's body, hanging under the oak, at Tom's body lying face down on the grass, and he knew they were not going to bury them. The hatred became a burning thing. No matter how contrary Tom had been, he was entitled to humane treatment. He tightened the *bayo's* cinch and got into the saddle.

· · ·

While Captain Duff was hunting down and shooting or hanging fifty more Unionists in that area, Talley pushed the *bayo* as hard as he could, and pulled into Austin late Monday afternoon. He stopped at the livery. "I lost a horse for you, Mumpy. I expect the Confederates have got it now. How much was it worth?"

"That horse? About thirty-five dollars—in gold."

"I'll pay you when I come back to town."

Mumpy Moore noted the salt on the barrel of the *bayo* around the saddle blankets, but he had seen Talley's face and said nothing.

Talley went by the post office. There was a crowd of men around it, as if they had never left it. B. B. Davis leaned against the front, his arms crossed over the barrel of a rifle whose butt rested on the board sidewalk.

Talley pulled up in front and sat for a moment, reading a poster, attached to the wall, addressed to the "People of Travis County," and signed, "F. A. J. Robertson, Captain, Quartermaster Corps, C.S.A."

"You come from the Nueces?" asked Abraham Tilden.

"Yes."

"Is it true—they killed the wounded?" asked Davis.

"They murdered them," said Talley in a hard voice.

"The telegraph said"—Davis was watching him carefully—"that they didn't even bury the dead."

Talley stared at him, and slowly shook his head. "They hanged Jim after he was wounded—and they didn't bury the dead."

Davis swore loudly and vehemently, in the manner of a man outraged but unable to do anything about it. There were growls from the men. Finally Davis said, "If I ever catch Duff alone, I'll kill him."

"You'll never catch him alone," Talley said. "He knows better."

"We could organize a posse," said Tilden.

"It wouldn't do a bit of good. He's got a hundred or more men, well-armed and well-equipped. Right now he's on the hunt for more Unionists, and I can tell you this: he'd welcome the chance to fight a posse—and he'd massacre them the same as he massacred the men on the Nueces."

"What are we going to do?" asked the telegraph man.

Talley roused himself. "Every man has to decide that for himself."

He rode slowly to the bank, left the *bayo* tied to one of the iron weights, and went upstairs to Robertson's office. The lines in the officer's face were deeper than usual, and in the half-light of the office his face looked gray.

"I was expecting you, Talley."

"I was on the Nueces," Talley said harshly. "I saw the whole thing."

Robertson studied him. "From your manner, it is evident the report is not exaggerated. I wish it were."

"What good is wishing?"

"None," Robertson admitted.

"They were my brothers," Talley said. "Tom and I fought, but he was still my brother. Jim was only sixteen—and I was watching when they hanged him."

"Will you sign a complaint?"

"What good are complaints? The boys are dead."

Robertson sat back. "There is something you should realize, Mr. Talley: not all of those on either side are what some of us would like them to be. I am sure that McCulloch and Hébert and the men over them will deplore this act as much as anybody else, but you must remember it takes time to iron out these things. In the meantime, such acts are being committed by individuals on both sides."

"Nothing," said Talley, "like this."

"I'm afraid you underestimate the rigors of war, Mr. Talley. My wife was hardly in her grave an hour," said Robertson, "when raiders—call them what you will; they raided in the name of the Union—struck my plantation, killed my three daughters, burned my house, took away my slaves. I too have a reason to be bitter, Mr. Talley, but I have tried not to be. I have tried to remember that neither side is fighting a holy war, and that neither army is made up of irreproachable men. I am sure that neither Jefferson Davis nor Abraham Lincoln would condone Captain Duff's actions, but in the meantime you and I are still alive, and we have our lives to live and our consciences to satisfy. It takes a great deal of understanding and patience, Mr. Talley, to be a citizen of any country."

Talley got up. "My patience is played out," he said, and left.

He ignored the men standing in silence outside. He strode to the *bayo,* swung into the saddle, and headed northwest at a hard lope. The sun was just setting when he slowed the *bayo* for the walk up the slope. The *bayo* was breathing heavily, and he patted it on the withers as he saw his mother in the door. But he rode to his own cabin and took off the saddle and took it inside. There was a double cartridge belt hanging from a peg on the wall. He took it down and saw that the front was filled with pistol bullets, the back with rifle bullets. He buckled it on, trying it. He put the pistol in the holster and tested the way it hung. He took the belt off and hung it over the peg. He cleaned his rifle and pistol and saw that they were loaded. He set the rifle on its pegs in the wall. His tin cup with the rawhide thong through the handle he hung on the saddle horn, and tied a hard leather *morral* on the side opposite the rifle's place—in front of his right leg. He went to the barn and got four pairs of rawhide hobbles and half a bushel of shelled corn in a tow sack and threw them all in a pile against the saddle. Then he went to the other cabin.

His mother watched him with dread in her eyes. He looked at her. "Ma," he said finally, "there's been some trouble."

Her eyes held his; her hands found the back of a chair. "Tom and—Jim?" she asked.

"Yes, Ma. They were with Tegener on the Nueces. Duff caught up with them."

"They were both—killed?"

"Yes, Ma."

He saw her face turning pale, and he put his hand awkwardly at her back. He would not tell her *how* they had died.

He ate cold cornbread and drank scalding coffee in silence.

His mother, wet-eyed but not crying, asked, "Where are you going, Roy?"

"I'm going to Mexico."

Her eyes dropped. She had anticipated this, he saw, but undoubtedly she had hoped against it. Now it had come and he felt sorry for her because she was helpless. "I'd like for you to go with me, Ma, and stay with Pa."

She shook her head slowly. "I'm too old to start

over again. A woman isn't made for work on the frontier after forty, Roy. Anyway, this is my home. I'm going to stay here."

"The Confederates will confiscate the ranch."

"I'll stay until they do," she said.

"Ma, aren't you at all mad about Tom and Jim?"

"I feel terrible," she said, raising her head, "but not mad. There is no good in madness over a thing like this. If the boys are gone, they are gone, and we have to think about those who are left."

"I see only one thing—"

"That's the trouble, Roy. War is a bigger thing than any of us. It causes terrible things not only because it's nation against nation but because it makes opportunities for men like Duff to do things they wouldn't dare to do in normal times. And it isn't limited to one side."

He watched her. That was what Robertson had said.

"For a lot of reasons," she went on, "I'm going to stay right here and see it through, no matter what happens."

"You can't run the ranch by yourself."

"I can hire help. I hope you'll leave me some of the money you brought back from New Orleans. I think I've earned it."

"Yes," he said, "I think you have. I'll leave you two thousand dollars. There's a good crop of calves and you can get plenty of credit at the bank."

Her eyes were fixed on his. "I'll have to start all over again. The bank will give me no credit without a man on the ranch. But never mind. I can still slop the hogs and brand calves and round up cows."

The next day he went about his business on the ranch and that day his mother had a chill. He saw her in bed with all the covers he could find, and two hours before sundown he got bridles and a rope and went after the *bayo* and three mules. He brought them to the cabin and saddled the *bayo*. He put the empty saddlebags on the mules.

"You're going early," his mother said.

"I changed my mind." He put an arm across her back and whispered to her, "The money will be in the old bee tree."

She nodded. "Write me a letter, Roy."

"I will." He got into the saddle. "Good-bye, Ma. I'll send somebody from Austin to look after you." He turned the *bayo* down the slope.

It was still not quite sundown when he stopped at the Garrisons'. Adele looked at the six-shooter on his hip. "You aren't going to try to find Duff?" she asked with alarm.

"Not right now. After the war I'll be back. If you're here then, I'd like to visit with you."

"You'll always be welcome, Roy."

He was glad she didn't insist on knowing what he was going to do.

"While I'm gone, I—Ma is having chills. Do you reckon—"

"I certainly will. I'll get a horse from Moore's and go out there tonight."

"I'm afraid she's having a relapse, but I couldn't get any quinine—and she can tell you what to do." He was more worried than he thought to be, but it wouldn't help any to hang around. Malaria was not a quick-acting disease anyway.

The Reverend Garrison worked his jaws. To Talley just then they seemed rather flabby than fat. "It's a terrible thing that has happened." He seemed a little dazed by it. "Surely this dark and monstrous deed will be repaid. 'Vengeance is mine, saith the Lord.'"

"I'm not asking the Lord to take my vengeance."

"Bloodshed will only bring more bloodshed."

Talley looked at him without seeing him. Vengeance might be measured in many ways—by the amount of gold drained out of the South, for instance, to pay for a drug that the South could not get along without.

Talley said harshly, "There are other ways to hurt the Confederacy more than going after the men who killed my brothers."

The Reverend didn't understand. He looked up

at Talley, but his eyes were vacant. "I will pray for you, my son," he said, and left the room.

Men watched Talley lead the mules along the streets of Austin but remained discreetly silent. Captain Robertson was waiting on the hotel step. As Talley approached, he stepped down to street level, and all the length of the street men turned to watch.

Talley's voice was flat. "Are you going to let me by, or are you going to try to stop me?"

Robertson's face seemed almost gray in the twilight. Finally he said, "I won't stop you, Talley; but this is dangerous ground you're treading. Military orders forbid anyone to leave this country for Mexico."

"The way I see it," Talley said coldly, "it's damned if you do and damned if you don't, and there is no choice for any of us."

Robertson looked beaten. He stepped aside, and Talley rode on.

CHAPTER XXII

AT THE MILLINERY SHOP Tally knocked on the outer door. He heard Helen Partridge's answer: "Just a moment." Then the door opened, and her dark face, dusky in the half-light, smiled at him. "I'm ready," she said.

He took the carpetbag. "You've got a pistol?"
"Yes."

"Not in here?"

"No."

"You may have to use it," he warned her.

"I'll be ready."

He led the way outside. He started up his string and rode past the *Bugle* office. He saw Mrs. Partridge, walking along the wooden planks, give Shelby a quick wave of her hand. He would not have seen it at all from his position, but the whiteness of her skin was reflected from the glass in Shelby's door. Shelby was sprawled out in the big chair and surrounded by a litter of papers. He made no move, but his eyes followed her until she passed from his sight.

Talley did some thinking. Mrs. Partridge was not a fool, but there were too many who had known ahead of time that she was taking a trip. Robertson had known it, for he had been waiting for Talley at the hotel door. Shelby must have known it, for he was entirely too casual. And of course Moore knew, at the livery. Perhaps the whole town knew. The best thing to do was get out of sight as soon as possible.

He stopped his string at the wide gate of the livery stable corral, and went into the shed with her. Moore was waiting; he looked at Talley but did not ask a question. A laden mule and a saddled horse were standing just inside the gate. Talley glanced at the bridles, tested the cheek straps. He examined the sidesaddle and tried the cinch. He made sure of the packsaddle and saw that the one saddlebag was fastened so it would not slide off. He stepped back.

"Any tricks to that mule?"

"He don't like coyotes, and if you hobble him you better crossfoot him."

Talley nodded. "He'll get used to coyotes before he gets back."

"Give him a long lead rope and you won't have any trouble."

They mounted, and Talley led off at a fast trot. Every head on the street was turned their way, but he did not look back. It was dark by the time they crossed the river, and he struck toward the south. The moon was rising higher on their left. They trotted steadily for an hour. Then Talley stopped and dismounted in the middle of an oak motte.

"Give the animals a breather," he said.

She got down slowly, but he did not offer her a hand. He was opening the saddlebag on her mule. He reached in, felt gold coins, took out a handful and looked at them in the moonlight. He dropped them back inside and heard dull clinks. He lifted the entire saddlebag, then buckled it tight and turned back.

She was in front of him. She said in a deadly voice that he had not heard from her before: "I might have killed you for that."

"If you hadn't had the gold," he said, "you would have *had* to kill me. As long as you did have the gold, you didn't dare, because you need me to get you across the border."

"Why did you look?" she demanded.

"Sometimes," he said, "I don't know who I'm playing with. When that happens, I like to be sure he's got money in the pot. I don't like for somebody else to gamble on my money."

"Don't you trust anybody?" she asked.

He could tell that for some reason she was interested in him for what he had done—but he didn't know the reason. "Yes, ma'am," he said, "there are some people I trust—when I know them real well."

"Don't you know me?"

"I can't say that I do—but I expect to know you before we get back from Mexico."

"I don't know about *your* money," she said, watching him.

"I expected forty thousand—but I'm a few hundred short. It couldn't be helped. Maybe we can do some fast talking in Monterrey. At worst, we can leave a few ounces there."

She did not answer, and he said, "Let's move on."

They rode across the flat country. At midnight he stopped to graze the animals in the bottom of a swale. He hobbled them while she waited, then gathered buffalo chips as big as a man's hat, but flat and light, and built a three-sided chimney. He put several handfuls of dried buffalo grass at the bottom, and used flint and steel to ignite the grass. The grass smoldered, and he fanned it with his hat until it broke into flame. He made coffee and got his tin cup from the saddle horn. He looked at her. She was standing and watching but not helping. He went to his blanket roll and pulled out a second tin cup.

"We were in such a hurry leaving New Orleans," she said, "I don't think I appreciated what an experienced traveler you really were. Where did you learn all these things?"

He studied her. "In the *brasada*," he said, "and on the *llano*."

They rested for an hour, then rode steadily until the moon was almost down. They crossed a stream, and he turned in the middle of it and rode down the bed for a mile, then pulled out at a rocky outcropping that crossed the stream at right angles. He let the animals stand on the rocks for a few minutes while the water ran off them; then he walked them off onto grass. He went over a hill and down a small canyon. He took off the saddlebags and hid them behind a group of green tumbleweeds beginning to turn purple. He hobbled the animals and turned them loose. He made coffee and some ash cakes, and they ate.

"How long will it take us to reach the border, traveling like this?" she asked.

He studied her. She had been unusually quiet during the night. "Eight days at this rate," he said.

She gestured at the animals, now grazing toward the east, where the sun would rise in half an hour. "You are very careful."

He stared at her. "There are a number who might follow us, and I think you know some of them."

She said coldly, "You aren't making this easy, Roy."

He put down his cup. "There's no way to make it easy. All I'm doing is making it possible."

They slept in snatches that day. It was a good valley, and the animals were tired and not inclined to wander. Toward sundown Talley roused himself from his blanket, built a small fire, then went to the stream and washed thoroughly.

When he came back, Mrs. Partridge was fixing up her hair. He mixed some corn batter and slid it into the hot ashes. He poured some water out of the can and made coffee. She did not offer to help with the chores. He was just sitting back on his heels when a voice sounded from above them on the opposite hill.

"¡Señores!"

"Venga," said Talley, but watched carefully as the tall straw-hatted Mexican made his way down the hillside toward them. He watched the top of the hill but saw no movement there.

The Mexican came up to their fire. He was middle-aged, with a long black mustache and a faded red sash around his waist. "I have seen one of your mules crossing the river down below, and have sent it back," he said.

"You know the brands?" Talley asked.

"*Si*. The R Bar T is an Austin brand."

At his side and a step behind him, Mrs. Partridge's hand went to her waist.

"Where do you come from?" asked Talley.

"I am work' for *Señor*—"

A pistol crashed in Talley's ear. He swung, crouching and drawing his six-shooter at the same time. There was a little cloud of smoke around Mrs. Partridge's head, and she held a .38 in her hand. The Mexican was on the ground beside the fire. Talley went to him. The man was on his face, his hat flattened against the ground. Talley turned him over. There was a tick in his shirt to the left of his breastbone. Talley ripped open his shirt and saw the small black spot on his chest. He felt for a heartbeat. There was none. He straightened the body and turned to Mrs. Partridge.

She still held the pistol, and her eyes were contemplative, as if she was waiting to see what he intended to do.

"You murdered him," he said at last.

She smiled. "You told me this was dangerous."

He did not like the smile. There was no amusement in it. "Put that thing away," he said. "Why did you shoot the Mexican?"

"You told me—"

"I said nothing about innocent Mexicans."

"I didn't know he was innocent."

"Look at him. Do you see any stirrup marks on those moccasins? He's probably a sheepherder—but you didn't waste any time killing him." He thought back. "You shot when he started to say he came from *Señor* Somebody. You were afraid he would tell a name that you didn't want me to hear."

She didn't answer. She still had the pistol in her left· hand.

He said slowly, "I didn't know you could kill a man so easily."

"What were you expecting as a partner in the smuggling business—a common milliner?"

He frowned. "I never gave it any thought."

She motioned with the pistol. "Get the mules loaded and let's get out of here."

He stared at her incredulously. Then his arm swept toward the pistol with all the strength he could put into it. The pistol exploded and his hand hit her wrist at almost the same time. The bullet cut a furrow on the inside of his left biceps; the pistol dropped into the rocks twenty feet away, and Mrs. Partridge held her arm and hand at an odd angle.

"You might have broken my wrist," she said.

"I might have broken your neck," he said.

He took his bandanna from around his neck to

bandage his arm. "Nobody orders me around at the point of a gun."

She tried to move her fingers. "My whole hand is numb," she complained. "I thought Texas men were chivalrous."

"I don't know about that, but I do know this: when a woman points a pistol at me, she's taking the place of a man and can expect to be treated like a man."

Her dark eyes were filled with hate. "A man would have killed you."

"Not unless he pulled the trigger quicker than you did."

"Don't you know I'll shoot you the first chance I get?"

He was emptying the coffee can. "No, you won't, for two reasons: first, you'll have to catch me with my back turned toward you, and I don't aim for you to do that. But most of all, you need me. You don't know anybody else who would get you across the border. Now go pick up your pistol. I'll get the animals."

He was grimly amused when he saw her mouth tighten. By now he had no doubt that she would shoot him the instant she no longer needed him. She did not know that he had plans of his own— and she was included in them only as far as Monterrey.

He turned the Mexican's body over so the buzzards could not get at the eyes.

• • •

By the time the moon rose, they had crossed the little canyon and cut back to the southwest to hit the main road.

"Isn't it dangerous to travel at night?" she asked.

"Not particularly. Anybody looking for you at night has to get pretty close to see you. In the daytime they can spot you miles away."

She was trying very hard to be pleasant. He noticed she favored her left hand, but he wasn't concerned. It would be that much less easy for her to point a pistol at him the next time. He did not take the pistol away from her, for she might need it, and, as he had said, she would not shoot him right away.

They entered the brush country and spent several days and nights crossing it. Now they traveled during the daytime, for trails were few, and it would not be easy for anybody trailing them to get ahead of them. The brush country was a wilderness of mesquite trees forty feet high, prickly pear cactus taller than a man on a horse, the *retama* with its yellow flowers, and the *tasajillo,* already showing its red berries that the quail and turkeys would eat during the winter. In here, a man could lose the trail in the daytime if he didn't keep his eyes open—and any man, on foot or on horseback, who tried to make his way through the chaparral on any other course than a trail, would be cut to pieces in half an hour by the diverse and multitudinous thorns—for the *brasada* was not a friendly place except to some birds and wood rats and snakes and razorback hogs and an occasional ocelot.

He shot a *javelina* one evening near sundown, and skinned it out and hung the meat in strips over the fire. He took the coffee can to look for water, for it was essentially a dry country, with few springs or running streams. When he came back and mixed the cornbread, he said, sitting cross-legged, "You see that thorn over there?"

"All I see *anywhere* is thorns."

"That's a special one," he said, pointing with his knife. "That's the *junco.* It never has any leaves, and the Mexicans say it is the kind that was woven into the crown of thorns worn by Christ when He was crucified."

She looked uncertainly at him. "What are you leading up to?"

"Just thought you would like to hear some of the local beliefs."

"I'm not interested in old wives' tales," she said sharply.

"There's only one bird will light on the *junco,*" he said thoughtfully. "That's the butcherbird."

She stared at him, and he knew she was scared of the brush. He shrugged it off. "People live in here," he said.

"That's impossible."

"No, I guess not. See any of these trails leading off to the side?"

"Not one."

"We pass one occasionally. They lead to a Mexican's *jacal,* or sometimes an outlaw camp," he said carelessly.

"Are you trying to frighten me?" she demanded.

"Not at all, ma'am." He stirred the coffee with his knife. "Just acquainting you with the country."

"And trying to prove how indispensable you are to me," she said with an unexpected burst of temper.

"Well, no, ma'am. It isn't that you have to have me—but you do have to have somebody, and it might as well be me, because it's just like you noticed: this isn't a friendly country unless you know it."

Unexpectedly she grabbed his arm, and for an instant he was alarmed, and then he was puzzled. But she bowed her head, and he felt tears soaking through his shirt sleeve, and knew she was crying. "I am afraid, Roy. I don't like the snakes or the cactus or the vultures. I'm glad I'm with you."

He patted her shoulder with the hand that had the knife in it. "Have a good cry," he said, "and get it out of your system—because it isn't any better on the other side of the border."

But he was glad when she quit crying and turned loose of his arm, for her fingers had dug into the furrow that her bullet had cut. It was healing well, but it was still mighty tender.

CHAPTER XXIII

THEY CROSSED THE RIVER two nights later, just about midnight, a little while before the moon came up.

"Are we near Edinburg now?" she asked as the horses felt their way in knee-deep water.

"No, ma'am, Edinburg is considerably east of here and some south."

She picked it up at once. "You told me we would cross at Edinburg."

"I changed my mind," he said.

He knew she was storing up all these things with every intention of paying him back with handsome interest.

They left the river and rode straight up into the desert country. He avoided the tiny settlement of Guerrero, and by morning they camped on a running stream. It would be, he told her, about three days more to Monterrey, which would bring them in on the twenty-fourth.

The country was arid, with scanty patches of buffalo grass, prickly pear from the small varieties that hugged the ground to giant trees covered with red or yellow flowers, and always *cholla,* the small, spine-filled cactus that seemed to be ubiquitous.

They traveled again in daylight, for, as Talley said, they were beyond the immediate danger area of *bandidos,* Union soldier-spies, and the possible far-riding Texas Rangers. They were in a country that he did not know as well as the brush country, and where traveling at night might draw more attention than traveling in daylight. Any obvious attempt at concealment, beyond those practiced by all travelers against the *léperos* or beggar-thieves, would be taken notice of and reported to bandit leaders.

They stopped that night at a small settlement composed of a very large building or cluster of buildings, a prominent adobe church topped with a cross, and half a dozen mud-brick *jacales* with reed-covered roofs.

"While we are in Mexico," Talley told her, "it would be best for me to be a *yanqui* and you an *inglesa*—Englishwoman—except of course in Monterrey, where you will be asked for your passport. There we will both claim to be English, but I will say that the Confederates took away my passport while we were trying to get out of Texas."

She watched him with steady eyes while she said, "My English passport has no Mexican visa."

It caught him off guard. "The hell you say!"

"The hell I do say," she answered quietly.

He was at a loss to interpret the emotion in her eyes and the strong word she had used. In Texas, women did not use those words, especially before men. But Helen Partridge, he realized, was like no woman he ever had known.

They pulled up to the *mesón,* where a young Mexican girl with long black hair hanging down to her shoulders, a white, low-cut blouse, a flowing yellow skirt, no stockings but neat and graceful shoes, was smoking a black cigaret as she sat on the stone step.

Talley stopped the *bayo* a yard away from her and asked, *"¿Está el mesoñero?"*

She scrutinized him with her liquid black eyes, and then examined Helen Partridge. Finally she nodded and said *"Sí,"* and disappeared within the open doorway.

Helen Partridge said, "She looks young—and innocent."

"She probably has a lover who would cut our throats for our mules," he said unemotionally, and looked at Mrs. Partridge. "It seems to be the peculiar ability of black-haired women to look young and innocent."

"I am not young," she answered, "and have never posed as innocent."

A pack of nondescript dogs came yapping around the corner and now worried at the animals' heels until a mule caught one in the flank with a hard hoof. The dog yelped, recovered his feet as soon as he hit the ground, and limped away, with the pack howling after him.

The *mesoñero* came from the opposite corner, followed by the *señorita,* who hung back a little, watching every movement and listening to every word.

"I am so sorry, *señor.*" He wrung his hands appropriately. "I was very busy directing the *mestizos* in an important project. May I be of service to you?"

It was obvious that he had just been awakened, but Talley merely said, "The *señora* and I wish accommodations for the night."

The *mesoñero* waved at the *mesón.* "It is very humble, *señor,* but I shall be happy to offer you my hospitality. You husband and wife, yes?"

"The *señora* is my sister. She is English; I am Yankee."

"*¡Inglésa!*" He bowed lower. "For you my very best accommodations, *señora.* You will please follow me."

The Mexican girl swung open a huge gate, and Talley rode through it with the mules, Mrs. Partridge following.

The corral or open yard was surrounded by a dozen or so mud-brick rooms with doors but no apparent windows.

"Will the animals stay in here?" asked Mrs. Partridge.

"No, there will be an outer yard for the animals,

but we'll unload here. Keep your eye on your saddlebag."

Two barefooted Mexican boys began to unpack the animals, and the harness and saddlebags and the rifle were taken, under the eye of both Talley and Mrs. Partridge, into one of the mud-brick rooms.

"You trust me with all the saddlebags?" she asked.

"Not any farther than a pistol shot," he said callously.

He saw that all their belongings were safe in the room, and the animals taken to water. Then the Mexican girl asked if he had any washing.

"No," he said, "but we are hungry."

She smiled and nodded vigorously. The *mesoñero* was weighing out corn for the animals, and the two servants carried straw to the stable.

Talley and Mrs. Partridge went to their rooms. She gasped. "There is nothing but a stone bed to sleep on."

"There are walls," he reminded her, "and within them we shall be safe from the *muy mal gente* who roam the *campo*. Likewise, our belongings will be safe as long as one of us watches them." He grinned sardonically. "And I have no doubt, *señora,* that you will watch them very carefully."

"I'd like to wash," she said coldly.

"Go out to the well. One of the servants will help you."

"The well is in the middle of the stable," she pointed out.

"Yes, of course. The *mesoñero* is more concerned with safety than with sanitation."

"What do you mean by that?"

"When the *Hacienda del Río Sarco* is besieged by Comanches or Apaches—which happens periodically—he can close the gates and mount men with rifles around the walls. With a well inside, they are secure from being starved out, since the Indians are not gifted with patience in these matters."

Not long after she returned, the Mexican girl brought a boiled chicken, an *olla* of *nacionales* or black beans with *chili colorado,* and a stack of *tortillas.* She seemed quite proud as she set this feast out on the stone floor.

But Mrs. Partridge was not enthusiastic. "I'd like to know," she said, "how I am expected to eat this mess without a fork or a spoon."

"Unnecessary hardware," he said cheerfully. "Take the *tortilla* thus." It was a very thin cake, and he held it on his thumb and middle finger while with his first finger he made a trough in it and scooped up beans. With his left hand he twisted a leg from the small chicken. "This is not Baltimore," he reminded her.

When it was dark, he said, "I'll sleep just inside the door, in case anybody should try to break in."

"It will also," she noted, "serve to keep me from

breaking out—for I have noticed that you sleep very lightly."

He grinned. "It is the only way to stay alive in this country."

Before daylight the *mesoñero* was knocking at the door with little cups of chocolate and sweet cakes called *bizcochos*. "I have also the bill for you, *señor.*"

"How much is it?"

"Board for one night, four reales each; hire of the room, four reales; one and a half *fanegas* of corn, one peso and two reales; straw for the animals, three reales. The total is three pesos and one real, *señor,* and I have the courage to hope the payment will be in gold."

Talley grumbled for effect. "You're all the same. By the time we get to Chihuahua we won't have a penny left."

After the *mesoñero* had gone, Mrs. Partridge asked curiously, "Why did you say 'Chihuahua'?"

"Because it is poor policy to say where you are really going."

"There's no place to go but Monterrey, is there?"

He shrugged. "No, but it helps to maintain the fiction of going somewhere else."

She said, puzzled, "I do not see what difference that could possibly make."

"It is a thing of Mexico," he said, and watched

her rubbing her shoulders and hips. "Soft bed, eh?"

She said something under her breath. He suspected it was blasphemy, and again it shocked him. "I never slept on rock before in my life," she said acidulously.

He watched her fix her hair back in place with the aid of a small mirror from her reticule.

Before sunup the *mesoñero* and his *mozos,* the slender barelegged girl smoking her cigarets, and most of the dogs of the *hacienda,* were out to see them off. Mrs. Partridge shuddered as they pulled out of sight down the winding trail. "I have never been in such a filthy place in my life."

"That's a woman's reaction," he observed. "They're very friendly people, really."

"You said they steal."

"Because they have to. After all, what are possessions? No one has them very long anyway. Besides"—he looked at her coldly—"is it worse to steal than to murder a man without reason?"

"You will go to the well once too often with that remark," she threatened.

Her eyes glinted, and he knew he had gotten to her that time. He knew too that she was capable of doing just what she implied. He must not forget that.

"Anyway," he said, hoping to turn it off, "by sleeping on bare stone you missed the fleas and bedbugs you would find if the *mesoñero* furnished the bedding."

Two hours later they entered a tiny village of a dozen adobe huts spread wide and lonely. Before one door was a small stool covered with a white cloth, and Talley said, "We'll stop here for breakfast."

"They have quaint customs," said Mrs. Partridge.

"They serve the purpose," he told her. "It is not the Mexicans' ways that are strange, but the travelers who are strangers to the ways."

At the *mesa puesta* they had eggs and *nacionales* with chili and garlic. The swarthy, smallpox-marked *señor* charged them four reales for the meal, and Talley haggled a little but paid it. "You can't pay without grumbling," he told her. "They would think you were in a hurry—perhaps running from the law."

She looked at him sharply, but said nothing.

CHAPTER XXIV

THEY KEPT southwest over narrow trails. The lower land was soil which seemed to support mostly cactus and a few goats; the upper land was rocky. They skirted the Picacho Mountains and came into Monterrey from the north.

It was in a fertile valley surrounded on all sides by the mountains of the Sierra Madre. The Rio

San Juan, as they approached, flowed from the mountains on the right, went around the town on the south, and curved back to the northeast. The town itself was rather neatly laid out in squares marked by hedges and irrigating ditches. The squares held scattered small adobe huts and large gardens, and in the canals were the inevitable girls and women bathing, notable at a distance from the flash of sun on olive-colored skin. They passed the citadel and went into the dusty main street, surrounded by yapping dogs and watched by myriads of small children and many bare-legged *señoritas* in doorways smoking brown-paper cigarets.

A sergeant in a uniform of oddments stopped them at the plaza. "You will report to the *capitán*," he said.

Talley glanced at the two equally ragged soldiers behind the sergeant and repressed a smile. "We have not come this long distance to talk with a *capitán*," he said. "We have a British passport."

The sergeant stiffened. He marched his detail back to the administration building in the plaza, and presently an older functionary came out. "You have the British passport, *señor?*"

"The *señora* has it."

She produced a heavy folded paper from one of her saddlebags, and he looked at the signature. Then he looked up sharply. "There is no visa, *señora?*"

"I am sorry," she said. "I had to leave New Orleans in such a hurry, I didn't have time."

"But you are Unionist. You could have waited until the Union navy—"

She shook her head sadly. "A city under attack is a city gone mad. One does not know whether to stay or go. If one stays, the Confederates may suspect one is awaiting the Unionists; if one flees, one is free."

He nodded slowly. "Perhaps it is so, *señora*. I suggest that you have your papers put in order at the first opportunity. And you, *señor?*"

"I am *inglés* also," Talley said, "and it is as the *señora* has said. They have stopped me to examine my passport and have taken it away from me." He smiled ruefully and showed the bullet furrow in the sleeve of his jacket. "I am lucky to get away with my life."

"You have come from New Orleans also?"

"Yes."

The *alcalde* smiled. "We have heard the Union navy conquered the city very quickly."

"I would like," said Talley, "to see the United States consul."

"Sí, señor."

"I would like also to have a detail of men to guard my animals while I am talking to the consul."

"But, *señor,* this is a peaceful city—"

"It is filled with refugees—Confederates,

Tejanos, Unionists, and spies for them all, including outlaws." Talley made a sweeping bow. "I know it is not your fault, *señor.* Such a great war is going on that no man can control the things that are happening. But I wish to have a guard, and will pay them well."

"In that case, *señor,* perhaps it can be arranged. It is true that we have many problems thrust upon us by the war in the north. And you, *señora,* you will go with your husband?"

She looked at Talley with a queer light in her eyes. "I require repairs to my saddle," she said without looking at the *alcalde,* "and I wish to buy a genuine Guatemalan *aparejo.* Can you direct me to a saddler?"

"Yes, *señora.*"

"I require the best in Monterrey," she told him. "I do not trust a clumsy-fingered workman. Is there a Don Agosto—?"

He glanced at the coin in her outstretched hand.

"*Pues, señora,* I think Don Agosto will be the one for you. I myself will show you where his shop resides. If you will but pardon me one moment, *señora,* I will obtain the guard to direct your husband to the consul."

He scurried into the courthouse, and Talley grinned at Mrs. Partridge, but there was no levity in her face. "I am going to find out if the quinine is ready for us," she said. "I will meet you at the market we passed in an hour."

He looked at the sun. "Make it two hours," he said. "This may take time."

"That will be satisfactory," she said, glancing at him.

CHAPTER XXV

PRESENTLY the *alcalde* came back with two soldiers. "They will guide you to the consul, *señor,* and will watch your animals as long as you require."

Talley gave each one a two-real piece. "There will be more for you when your work is finished," he said.

"*Bien, señor.* We watch them very well indeed."

"All right, lead on."

The consul's office was over a bank, but the consul was not in, said the clerk. "He's away in Saltillo, checking up on some refugees. Is there anything I can do? My name is Premont."

Talley pushed his hat back. "Do you keep informed on the Texas Unionists who come here?"

"We try to. Whom do want to find?"

"Talley—Robert Talley. He's my father."

Premont brightened. "Talley? He's been expecting you for some time." He stepped back and studied Talley. "You look alike."

"He has gray hair."

"That's Robert Talley, all right. I was a little doubtful at first. We have to watch these Texas men, you know."

"I know. And my father?"

"You will find him at a *mesón* called Los Pascualitos, two blocks west and two blocks north. He is working as a tanner."

"A tanner?"

"There have been so many, we couldn't provide more than necessities. We enlisted all who wished in the Union army, but your father insisted on waiting for you."

"Thanks. I'll look him up now."

"What's your first name?"

"Roy."

Premont said thoughtfully, "Talley—Roy Talley." He opened a drawer of his desk. "Got a telegram for you a couple of days ago." He opened another drawer and tossed out a square sheet of white paper with black printing across the top. The message was written in black ink across the middle: "Your mother had a relapse Kenedy says only hope is medicine. Adele."

He folded it slowly and put it in his shirt. Adele was telling him they needed quinine. This was no trick of his mother's, for she would never resort to anything like that. If her men didn't stay with her, she carried on by herself. But Adele had found out that his mother wasn't sure he was coming back, and had taken this means of letting him know she needed quinine. He moistened his lips slowly and at last looked up.

"Thanks."

He was a little anxious about his saddlebags. He got outside and saw that they were all right. Then he mounted the *bayo* and went to the *mesón* Los Pascualitos.

He inquired of the *mesoñero*. "Oh, *sí*." The *mesoñero* was happy to show him where the *señor* Talley stayed.

Talley saw that the mules came inside the yard. He admonished the two guards to watch the animals, and followed the *mesoñero* to find his father. They went through the stable and toward a small canal. There, lying on a blanket in the shade of a gnarled cedar tree, was his father, taking a siesta.

"Roy!" He jumped up. "Roy! How are you!"

"Fine," said Talley. "You look older, Pa."

"I *am* older. It has been almost a year—and a hard year."

"You are working?"

His father shrugged. "Enough to live—and wait. I have some *pulque* inside. Would you—"

"I don't have time right now."

"You are by yourself?"

"I am with a woman who has a British passport—but without a Mexican visa, as I just learned. However, I think from the looks of the *alcalde* we'll get along all right."

"You don't need a passport now anyway. If you have money—"

Roy told him about the quinine.

"The money you get for it will be a fortune in this country."

"Yes," Roy said slowly, "but there's more to it. Mother was taken with the chills just before I left—and there's no quinine in Texas."

His father did not seem to be disturbed by the information. "She's had 'em before," he said, "and pulled through all right."

Roy looked at him sharply, then sat on his heels on the hard ground, his back against the cedar tree. "Have you found a ranch we can buy?"

"Yes, over in Tamaulipas."

"Why not here?"

"I had a chance to cultivate the governor over there and give him some advice. If he puts down the revolution, we can get a large ranch for almost nothing."

"And if he loses?"

His father shrugged. "We'll go to Sonora—Guaymas, maybe."

Talley frowned. "Why not here?" he asked again.

His father said, "I've been here a year already."

"A little south of here we would be safe from Indians."

"No, I think Sonora is better. It's a newer country. You can get more land cheaper over there."

That rang a familiar note in Roy's thoughts. "But Sonora—the Indians are still bad over there, and the government is even more distant from Mexico City. What about revolutions?"

"Revolutions?" His father smiled dreamily. "Then we'll go somewhere else. The world is big—"

Talley was beginning to feel uncomfortable. "Where else?"

"Oh, Venezuela, Argentina—anywhere where there is land and freedom."

"And if it happens again in Venezuela?"

"Africa, maybe—or India. I tell you it's a big world, Roy. There is no limit—"

Talley said slowly, "I always wanted to get the family back together—all in one house. I wanted to get where mother wouldn't have to work so hard."

"Sure," said his father, yawning. "Sure, we'll—"

"How many more pioneer ranches do you think mother can live through?"

"Well, yes, I suppose—but then—"

Roy's eyes were narrow. "Mother said you were always on the move whenever you disagreed with the majority."

His father looked at him warily.

"I think maybe you've deliberately put yourself with the minority because you got tired of staying in one place," said Roy.

His father frowned. He was about Roy's size,

266

compact, small-boned, but with eyes that never quite let a man look inside of them. "You've got something on your mind, Roy."

"I've been sitting here trying to figure it out, and I see now what's wrong. Mother was right: a man doesn't jump the traces every time he's in the minority. He stays and sees it through. If the government's bad, he puts his shoulder to the wheel and makes a good government out of it."

"And so—"

"You didn't do that. You made a lot of high-sounding talk about freedom—*but you cut and run.*"

His father's eyes were narrow. "A man doesn't have to live in a country that he doesn't—"

"You—and others like you—have done terrible damage to Texas. I don't say you meant to, but that's the way it turned out."

"I don't know what you're talking about."

"Tom—Tom was a weakling. He tried to be hard to make up for his lack of judgment. He looked to you when he didn't know what to do. He did what he thought you would do."

His father shook his head. "This has nothing to do with me leaving Texas."

Roy got to his feet. "It has everything—because Tom tried to leave Texas too—he and Jim together."

"They could have done worse than stay and take abuse—"

"Could they?" asked Roy. "Tom and Jim joined a company going to Mexico. They were caught on the Nueces and massacred by Confederate soldiers."

"That proves it!"

"It proves something else to me," Roy said hotly. "It shows me now that *I* was crossed up. I came after quinine to take revenge on the Confederacy, when it's really Duff I should be after. War is war, and a lot of personal injustices are bound to happen, but we've got to stick to the big thing. Men who should be leaders have got to go along with the majority. When they don't, young boys like Tom and Jim get the wrong ideas—and they get caught, because no government is going to stand for defiance. Venezuela or Africa or India would require allegiance—and you'd have to give it or run."

"It is our right to run."

"Your right," said Roy, "but not your privilege—not in time of war."

"Then," his father said triumphantly, "you admit we had no right to secede in the first place!"

"Maybe not. I don't know. But I do know one thing—you built up a fortune in Texas, and you owed something to the state. If its leaders made the wrong move, you had a duty to stay and try to straighten them out. But above all, you had a family there. You had no right to pull out for Mexico and leave us by ourselves."

His father stood up. "No right?" he asked softly.

Roy hesitated. "You left your family and your land behind."

His father's eyes were narrow. "You're flustrated now because your mother needs some quinine. But I tell you, Roy, there'll be a million like her in the South this fall."

Roy studied him for a moment. "Yes, perhaps a million," he said softly, "and every one of them will suffer—and many die—if the quinine isn't there."

There was a peculiar light in his father's eyes. "I've been depending on you to sell the ranch and bring the money here so we could start over."

Roy said stubbornly: "The land is in Texas and my mother is in Texas, and I'm going to stay in Texas. If you want us, you can come back home."

His father looked at him a long time. "You're hard," he said. "I always knew you were the hard one."

"Maybe I'll see you," Roy said quietly.

"You've forgotten one thing." His father's voice was cold. "You've got forty thousand dollars of my money."

"It isn't your money. It's family money."

"I made it!" His father's eyes were blazing.

"No, we all made it—mother and me and Tom and Jim. You can't rightly claim more than a fifth of it."

"Then give me my fifth."

Talley was shocked. "You'd take your fifth and drop out—like that?" He took a deep breath. "The money stays in the family!"

His father advanced. "Give me my share!" he ordered.

Roy didn't move. "Not unless you can take it away from me."

For a moment he thought his father would make a play, and he would have admired him more if he had. But his father looked at his eyes and slowly changed his mind.

"Run where you wish," said Roy. "I'm going back to Texas and operate the ranch. If you want any part of it, you will have to come back. But we aren't waiting. We're going to work for the Confederacy. They need quinine right now, and I'm going to see they get it. Later on, if the Confederacy loses, we'll work for the Union. Whatever happens, we won't run."

"There'll be tough times if the Union wins."

"We'll live through them." He half turned. "So long, Pa."

He strode back to the gate of the *mesón*. He was so wrought up emotionally he didn't notice anything wrong until he reached the *bayo*.

One of the guards was sitting with his back against the adobe wall, and a wound on his hatless head bled freely. The other, lying at full length on his face in the dust, did not move.

"*¡Carajo!*" shouted the *mesoñero*.

Talley glanced at the mules. The saddlebags were gone. For a moment his lips tightened. Then he turned the fallen soldier over on his back. He saw no wound, but the Mexican seemed to be unconscious. He started to feel inside the Mexican's *serape,* and the man came to life immediately, protesting.

"*No, señor. ¡Por favor, no!*"

Talley ran to the street and looked up and down but saw no one. He went back to the Mexican, who was getting up.

"Who took them?" Talley demanded. "Who took the *alforjas?*"

The Mexican shook his head solemnly "I do not see anybody, *señor.*"

Talley shook him by the front of his shirt. "Who took them? Who took them?"

The Mexican's feelings seemed to recede into the depths of his eyes. He said as from beyond a door, "*No sé señor, no sé.*"

Talley felt like taking a swing at the man, but he knew it would not do any good. "Get some water!" he barked at the *mesoñero*.

"*Sí señor.*" The *mesoñero* scurried away while Talley glanced at the mules. The straps had been cut clean, and the buckles were still fastened to the rings. The *mesoñero* came back and splashed a cowhide container of water in the injured man's face. Talley bent down to him.

"Who hit you, *soldado?* Who struck you?"

The man looked dazed. He put one hand to the top of his head and felt the blood. His eyes widened. He looked at the blood and then at Talley.

"I do not see anyone, *señor.* I am standing here watching the *machas* when suddenly I feel a great jar on the top of my head and everything blackens and I fall down and that is all I know."

"All right." Talley bent over. "Where was this other fellow when you were hit?"

"He was watching the street, *señor,* while I was watching the *machas,* and then—"

Talley straightened. "I know what happened then."

"You can buy more saddlebags, *señor,*" said the *mesoñero,* "from the saddlemaker down by—"

"Saddlebags?" Talley stared at him. He mounted the *bayo.* "You better get that man to a doctor!" he shouted.

"*Sí, señor,* he shall have the best."

Talley rode out. He had turned his back on Mrs. Partridge; he had denied his own father; he had lost the gold. And he was in a foreign country without a passport.

He galloped back to see Premont, the Union consul, and told him about the loss of the gold. He said only that he had been fleeing from Texas—not that he had changed his mind.

"I'm sorry, Mr. Talley. There is not much we

can do. It is a period of upset, and many extra-legal activities are focused in Monterrey. I have no doubt the man in charge, the one who was watching the street, was bribed to allow somebody to get your saddlebags."

"It was done so fast, though."

"It doesn't take long. A couple of gold pieces."

"I gave him—"

"To a Mexican, money is money, especially if it comes from a Yankee or a possible Texan." He was thoughtful. "You had been in town only a short while, hadn't you?"

"Half an hour or so."

"It rather seems that somebody knew exactly what you had in the saddlebags," said Premont. "There is so much smuggling, and mule trains arrive constantly from Laredo and Reynosa. The Mexican republic has given strict instructions that such trade must be stopped, but—" He shrugged.

"Wait a minute!" Talley pushed his hat back on his head. "The one who came with me from Texas—"

"Yes, of course. Can you describe him?"

"It wasn't a him. Look!" He seized Premont by the shoulders. "Where would you go to get delivery of quinine?"

"Quinine? Oh, I see. The saddlemaker, Don Agosto, I think, is the most likely."

"But wait now. She'd have to buy mules."

Talley turned loose of his shoulders. "Where would a mule train leave the town? She'd have to have a guide."

"I think that could be had very quickly—at a price. And mules also."

"She could pay the price."

Premont nodded. "Go back to the citadel. A little beyond it you will find an open place where you can watch all roads to the northeast."

"How about the road to Laredo?"

"You can cover that too. There is a bridge over a small stream that runs into the river, and the roads to the north go across it."

"That leaves how many roads open?"

"The west road to Saltillo and the south road to Mexico City."

"How about the Saltillo road?"

"Not likely." He traced out the road on a map on the wall. "There is not much possibility of cutting across the mountains without undue risk. Going on to Saltillo, you would have to go up to Piedras Negras. It can be done, but it is twice as far. No, I think if I were in her shoes I would try to get out of town to the north or east."

Talley studied the map for a moment. Then he pulled his hat down hard on his head. "That's what she would do. She wouldn't dare run the mountains with $60,000 worth of quinine."

"Perhaps—"

"Thanks, Premont. Thanks a lot."

He was out, down the rickety stairway, and into the saddle. He galloped north past the citadel until he found a high spot from which he could watch all roads while he kept his animals concealed below him.

Within a quarter of an hour he saw her, making the big gamble, coming back along the way they had entered Monterrey. A man on horseback was ahead; three pack mules followed him, and Mrs. Partridge, unmistakable from her sidesaddle posture, brought up the rear. They were traveling at a trot.

He went down the hill on foot, mounted the *bayo,* and skirted the hill to reach the road. He sat the *bayo* beneath a large oak tree in a grove until the train was fairly close. Then he trotted out of the trees and took the road to meet them.

For a moment he was unchallenged. Then Mrs. Partridge must have identified the *bayo naranjado,* for she shouted something at the guide and at the same time reached for her .38. But Talley was holding his .41 on the guide, who now, thoroughly confused and much preferring to lose Mrs. Partridge's cargo rather than his life, did nothing.

"¡Arriba!" shouted Talley, and the guide raised his hands slowly but carefully. Talley had kept him between Mrs. Partridge and himself, and now he said, "Go back to Monterrey, *hombre.*"

The Mexican lowered his hands slowly. "But my pay, *señor.* She promised—"

"Pay him," Talley ordered.

It was hard to fathom the emotions that stirred in her eyes, but Talley was not particularly interested in what she thought. He held his .41 where he could cover the two of them. He didn't think the Mexican would risk his hide, but he wasn't going to take a chance. He watched her pay him, and yelled "Now vamoose!"

The Mexican left toward Monterrey at a hard gallop. Talley said to Mrs. Partridge, "You've just hired a new guide."

The muscles worked around her mouth and her eyes were filled with venom, but she said nothing.

"You go ahead," he ordered.

She walked her horse slowly past the mules.

"You would stab your own mother in the back," he said. "You would get back to Texas and haggle with Confederate officials over the last ounce of flesh. You'd get a thousand dollars an ounce for this stuff if you could." He went on, thinking about it. "I ought to take that six-shooter away from you," he said. "But on the other hand, you're so damned clever with it that I'd better let you keep it. We've got a long way to go, and that pistol might do some good. If anybody holds us up, they will watch me for gunplay—not you. In that case you might be able to save the quinine for us." He didn't add that he planned to take the pistol away from her as soon as they got within striking distance of Austin.

She was silent for a moment. Then she said, "If you feel so bitter about me, why not shoot me now and have it over with?"

He grinned. "You know I wouldn't, or you wouldn't say that. You're a woman and I've never shot a woman—but don't misunderstand me; I will if you force me. Besides, I may need you to get us across the border. I don't know what your connection is with the Confederacy or the Union but you've got one with both of them. So you're still alive but you're on good behavior."

She rode off up the dusty trail without a word.

"And don't grind your teeth," he called after her. "It bothers the mules."

In the United States consul's office the guide was reporting to Premont. Premont listened thoughtfully and went to the map. "They can't possibly get farther than Pesquería tonight," he said. "I want you to take the trail from Apodaca to Marín, and cut back to the Roma road. Take an extra horse so there will be no slip-up." He turned on the Mexican. "How much was there in his saddlebags?"

A man entered from the back room. He was a fat man, and he was brushing the tip of his nose with a blue bandanna handkerchief. "We want that quinine to go to the Confederacy for sure," he said. "We want their gold. We want them to pay through the nose for it."

"We'll get the quinine delivered," said Premont. "How much did you say was in the saddlebags, Manuel?"

"Thirty-five thousand, *señor.*"

"You're a liar. He told me forty thousand."

The Mexican's eyes were wide—too wide. Premont said, "I will give you a hundred dollars if you do this job right."

"I will work *muy bien,* señor."

"It's in quinine now, but that's better than gold. Get to the border and go to Austin. We have a Union agent there named Shelby, who runs the newspaper in Austin. Get to him as soon as possible and tell him those two are on the way north with three thousand ounces of quinine."

"I do not understand, *señor.* Why do you not let me capture the quinine before they get to the border?"

Premont said harshly, "We *want* the quinine to go north. Shelby and his men can take the quinine from Talley before he reaches Austin and then sell it to the Confederacy for half a million dollars—in gold. When all their gold is gone, the Confederacy cannot make war any longer, for it requires gold to buy the many things they need." He paused. "No agricultural country should ever try to make war."

"I am to tell him this and then return?"

"Get there as soon as possible. It will take time for him to act."

"Sí, señor." The Mexican left. He would have time for a glass of that heavenly *pulque,* for a train of six horses and mules could not travel fast. Strange indeed, he thought, were the ways of the *norteamericanos.* Even more than the Mexicans, the *norteamericanos,* the *yanquís,* the *burros,* could not be trusted. A Mexican would cut your throat, of course, but then you expected that of a Mexican. The *norteamericanos,* on the other hand, were sometimes loyal, sometimes not. You could never tell. Just when you thought they were childishly simple and trusting, they turned out to be *muy coyote*—clever in a high degree. Well, he shrugged, it was a *cosa de México*—one of those things. Not his worry. With *bastante pulque* and a long parade of black-eyed *señoritas,* it would be weeks before he would need to worry. And all because of the peculiar double standard of the *norteamericanos.* . . .

Talley stopped at the *mesón* at Pesquería that night, just as Premont had foreseen. He took the saddlebags with their treasure of quinine into the room as he had done before. He had nothing to fear from Mrs. Partridge until they got through the brush country. Between Pesquería and that point, she did not dare to leave him.

The next morning before sunup they were on the way, fortified with coffee and the inevitable *bizcochos*. They skirted the Picachos that night and stopped at a *rancho* near a small town. The next night they were at the *Hacienda del Río Sarco,* half a day's ride from the river. He pulled away from the trail and cut across the arid country northwest.

"We'll cross the river at a new place," he said. "Somebody may be waiting for us at the other place."

He began to watch the sky to the northwest, for it was almost September, and already he had seen cranes flying south. It was early for bad weather, but it might rain at any time, and at this period of the year any rain might turn into a cold norther.

He rode parallel to the river, staying back in the scanty chaparral and out of sight as much as possible, until he located a rock shelf on which they could cross to the north, and he turned the train toward it.

Mrs. Partridge's horse was picking its way among the loose rocks when three men stepped into view from behind a thick screen of mesquite. Talley was in the rear, but he heard a voice say, "Mrs. Partridge! I hardly expected to see you here!"

Talley frowned and stopped his horse. The leader was a man with a dun-colored beaver hat and a fancy vest. He held a big cigar in the very middle of his mouth, and spoke around it.

Mrs. Partridge pulled up sharply and said, "Why are you here, *Señor Díaz?*"

Talley's hand rested on the butt of his pistol. He had heard panic in her voice, and he sensed that whatever was about to happen was not of her doing.

"You found the cargo as I promised, *señora?*"

"Yes—and paid for it."

"*Bien, bien.* You will now dismount and turn your horse over to my men."

"Traitor!" she cried.

He said insolently, "Perhaps it depends on which side of the fence you are on, *señora.* From my side, it is you who are a traitor."

She began to argue. "You cannot take this away from me. I paid for it, and if you hold me up, nobody else will do business with you."

"For half a million dollars, *señora,* I can forego that pleasure. Besides, I don't anticipate that you will tell anybody what has happened on the Rio Grande."

As so many men must have done before, he had underestimated her. She made as if to dismount, and half-turned her back. Then she straightened, her .38 blazing.

Three bullets struck him in the chest. He stood there a moment, his swarthy, cynical face showing a moment of disbelief. Then he collapsed.

Talley slammed his heels into the *bayo's* flanks, and the horse leaped forward. Staying low on the horse's neck, he shot twice at the man on the right. The man fell over backward, his arms flung out. The other man had fired three shots, but now hesitated, and Talley straightened so he could see him, and put two bullets into his stomach as the man was trying to aim the pistol. The man doubled over and fell on his face.

Talley circled back and watched them for a moment. He was bleeding a little from a crease on the right shoulder, but it wasn't serious. He got down, his .41 ready, and examined the man Mrs. Partridge had shot. The cigar had fallen out of his mouth and had been crushed by his body; the man was dead. The one lying on his back was dead. The one on his stomach was moving his head from side to side, pivoting on his forehead, and moaning. Talley turned him over. He wouldn't last long, for blood was pouring from his mouth.

Talley looked up at Mrs. Partridge. "You always shoot to kill, don't you?"

"Always," she said, still holding the .38 in his general direction.

Talley held the .41 on her.

"What if I tell you to give me your pistol?" she asked.

He knew she was testing him. He said, "I would shoot you between the eyes. I have one bullet left, Mrs. Partridge."

He watched her hide the .38 at her waist. "Who's your friend?" he asked.

"He is the man I made arrangements with in San Antonio," she said.

"Nice fellow. He'd cut your throat with a saw-tooth cactus."

She said with distaste, "He was not a man to rely on."

He looked at her and snorted. Letting her keep the pistol had worked out fine. He pointed with the .41 at the river. With her lips tight, she led off. The water was only knee-deep, and the mules gave no trouble. When they reached the middle of the stream, Talley reloaded the .41 and followed.

What she felt for him surely was not hate, for that was too personal. In her eyes he was plainly like a snake, something to be killed from force of habit, and it was with a certain smug amusement that he contemplated their approaching settlement with each other somewhere beyond the brush country.

By the evening of the next day they were in the *brasada*. It was good weather and the coyotes were singing at twilight at the top of every rise. The threat of a norther seemed to have disappeared, and sometimes during the sunny part of the day they could hear a canyon wren running lightly down the scale.

That night they ate *carne asada* or dried beef,

with coffee made from their canteens, while the animals browsed on the soft *huajilla* cactus that smelled like balsam. The prickly pear was as high as a tree; the *retama,* the *agarita,* the *vara dulce* and the *amargosa* surrounded them.

"The chaparral seems to grow in toward us," Mrs. Partridge said, looking at the forbidding green tangle distastefully.

Talley made a place in the fire for the coffee can. "I never figured you as imaginative," he observed.

"I can be glad of one thing," she said after a moment. "Even though you don't trust me, you know the country."

He looked at her contemplatively. "Mrs. Partridge," he said, "after seeing you kill that harmless Mexican south of Austin, I could travel with you for a thousand years—but I would never trust you."

Saying this, he had declared himself, and he felt better although he realized that he had put her on guard. But he wouldn't worry about that; she was very quick with that .38, but he was as fast and certainly stronger.

Halfway through the brush country they came to a clearing at the edge of a small swamp, and a very brown Mexican in straw hat, shirt, and pants came to meet them. "Don Roi!" he exclaimed. *"Me da tanto gusto de ver á Vd."*

Talley got off the *bayo* and hugged the

Mexican. "*Hace mucho tiempo*. It is a long time," he said.

Miguel had a pretty little wife named Carmen and three small brown children. Carmen, also barefooted, wore a simple dress that had been so ripped by thorns that it barely covered her; the children wore nothing.

They had a good supper of *nacionales* with much chili and plenty of rank-tasting goat meat.

"You like it here, Miguel?" Talley asked as Carmen nursed the youngest baby after supper.

"Sure. Why not? I have no worries."

Mrs. Partridge shuddered inwardly. "But you are so far from stores," she said.

"*Es nada.* It is nothing, *señora*. Stores are to make you want more than you need. What more can we need than we have here? We have clothes enough for the decencies. We have plenty food. We raise beans and chili and let the goats run wild. Sometimes I catch a deer. At night we sit very quiet in the door in the moonlight and watch the great *ladiños*—the wild outlaw steers—come down to drink. Of what use is money if only to buy things one does not at all need?"

Talley glanced at Mrs. Partridge's face in the glow of the mesquite-root fire. She was watching Carmen and the baby with an odd expression.

"Once in a while," Miguel went on, "I make the trip to Laredo. We have a tame burro down in the *arroyo,* and we all go into town. We buy a little tobacco, some sugar, a piece of ribbon, some powder and lead for my old rifle." He looked proudly at the ancient muzzle-loading *escopeta* hanging on pegs in the wall. "It is a very fine rifle, *señor.* My grandfather used it against the Lipan Apaches. At that time the Apaches had only bows and arrows, and my grandfather was able to take many scalps, and the Indians came to have a great superstition of him."

"Do the Lipans ever come around here?" asked Talley.

"*Sí,* they come but they do not harm us. They know I have the rifle, and they fear it as bad medicine."

"You use it sometimes?"

"Once in a while I kill a wild hog for us to eat, or to take the meat and hide to trade for things we need."

"And *pulque?*"

"Ah, Carmen makes the finest *pulque* in the land—from *nopal,* the prickly pear."

Talley glanced at Carmen. Her black eyes were bright with pride at Miguel's mention of her. She put the baby in her other arm to change breasts.

"You have everything you want," said Talley.

"*Por supuesto*—of course. To know the *brasada* is to love it, *señor,* and here come no tax collectors, for nobody will travel this far through the thorns to get a few pennies."

The next morning they slept late, for Miguel

and Carmen were in no hurry to get up. They had beans and goat meat, topped off with *queso de tuna,* which Miguel proudly explained was Carmen's special dish—prickly pear apples preserved.

After breakfast Miguel insisted that they stay for a smoke, and Talley consented, partly because he saw it was annoying to Mrs. Partridge. He and Miguel sat outside in the shade of a cactus thatch, while Mrs. Partridge, with a tight look on her face, waited impatiently alongside the mules. The children played in the brush, sometimes quietly, sometimes noisily. Carmen, with a root of *amole* which Miguel had found for her, went down to the water, chased away a coyote hunting frogs, and washed her hair thoroughly in an abundant lather that left her hair gleaming softly and with unexpectedly lovely fragrance. Talley gave Miguel a pound of tobacco, and smoked a cigaret with him.

At last, by mid-forenoon, Talley rose and thanked Miguel. Carmen was sitting in the doorway with her black hair spread out in the sun. Talley got on the *bayo* and Mrs. Partridge led off.

At the first breather she expressed her vexation. "I thought you would never leave those filthy Mexicans."

"Filth," said Talley, "is a matter of taste. To some people, filth can be as much in the mind as in the body. But come to think of it, did you ever see a woman's hair any cleaner or prettier than Carmen's?"

He was thinking of Adele Garrison as he said it, for her hair too had that distinctive fragrance of good health and cleanliness, and he remembered it as one of the things that had attracted him to her. He looked at Mrs. Partridge. "There wasn't any hurry, was there?"

She answered coldly, "With a fortune in quinine, you dawdle over cigarets with a Mexican." She shuddered delicately. "They live like animals!"

He said with calculation, "Maybe you don't like to see people be happy with so little when you are not happy with so much."

They spent one more night in the brush country, and then the prickly pear got smaller, the patches of grass grew larger, and the rank forest of cactus began to recede.

"Where will we come out?" she asked.

"We'll hit the road just north of Beeville. I know another Mexican up there, and we may be able to get news."

"I will not," she said positively, "spend another night in a Mexican hut."

"It won't be necessary. Felipe's wife died of the *vómito* some years ago, and he has lived alone ever since. Anyway," he said cheerfully, "we'll hit his place about noon."

Felipe was older. He herded a few goats and lived in a tiny hut with pictures of the Christ and the Virgin Mary on the walls. He insisted they eat, and Talley suppressed a grin as he watched Mrs. Partridge's eyes narrow over the inevitable beans and goat meat, with no fork or spoon but only the thin tortillas with which each person dipped into the same pot. They sat on the floor, the men cross-legged, Mrs. Partridge with her legs disposed under her, and it was obvious that she was nearing the end of her patience with him.

"*Señor*," said Felipe, "there is something I think you should know."

"Perhaps you will enlighten me."

Felipe cupped a tortilla around his index finger. "Men were here yesterday, inquiring about you."

"From which direction did they come?"

"From south."

"How many men were there?"

"Four."

"Well-mounted?"

Felipe dipped into the beans. "*Sí, señor,* very well mounted."

"And they asked—?"

"They want to know if a man and *mujer* with so many several pack mules have come this way. And I have said no, I do not see them."

Talley nodded gravely. "And they rode away to the north?"

"*Sí, señor.*"

"Can you describe them?"

"The two *jefes, señor.* One is big, roughly dressed and loud speaking, and wears a black beard. He is the one who threatened me with a knife—but what could I say, *señor?* I have wanted to say what will please him, but he has said he will return, so I must tell him the truth. *¿Verdad?*"

"It is the only answer. And what of the other man?"

Felipe concentrated. "He is—let me remember—he is a big man also, perhaps bigger. He is of brown hair; he slouches and seems very careless, and he talks with a sound like a snake hissing."

Talley looked full at Mrs. Partridge, and was astonished at what he saw. He had anticipated that she had made arrangements with someone to meet them and either rob them or kill him; he had supposed that was why she had been impatient at the delay in the brush. But perhaps he had done her an injustice, for there was no question that this news was a shock to her. She stared at Felipe, disbelief in her eyes, and then her glance flashed to Talley. She saw his eyes full upon her, and he knew that if she had expected to meet anyone it was neither Joe Cooper nor Hugh Shelby. Now he knew beyond question it was best to let her keep her pistol until the last day.

She asked breathlessly, "What are we going to do?"

"Keep on," he said. "If they've come down here looking for us, they won't give up until they find us."

"Couldn't we go around?"

"Go around to where? Eventually we have to go to Austin."

"We could go east to Houston."

He considered. "They will be hunting us, and that means they've got people like Felipe keeping their eyes open in all directions."

"We could reach Houston before word gets back."

"You forget the telegraph."

"You want to keep straight on?" she asked.

"I think it best."

"It will mean a sure fight."

"At least we'll know from which direction to expect it."

She said slowly, "I wish you would remember that you are risking my entire fortune."

"You forget," he said, eying her, "that my money paid for two thirds of our fortune."

"Well, yes, of course," she said hastily.

After dinner she went down to the creek to wash, and Felipe and Talley settled down for a smoke. They rolled cigarets. Felipe took from his shirt pocket a wadded-up piece of buckskin. He opened it, revealing a short red cord of tinder, a steel *eslabón,* and a small piece of flint. He struck a spark into the tinder and blew on it until it flamed. He lighted both cigarets, then blew the fire out, rewrapped all the items in the buckskin, and put the package back in his shirt pocket.

"*Señor,*" he said, "this woman is not your wife?"

"No."

"I would say something to you, *señor,* about her."

"I'll listen."

"I am an old man," said Felipe. "I was an old man when you were born—an event I well remember. I have sometimes been known as a *miramuerte*—a death-seer, a prophet—but it was not a power I wanted, and I have not cultivated it. But I have a feeling here, *señor,* and in respect to your mother I must tell it to you."

"Yes," said Talley, watching him through the smoke of the cigaret.

"This *señora*—she is not good; she is evil. There is death around her."

Talley said gravely, "That I have seen."

"But there is more to come, *señor.* The coldness of death is in her eyes, in her stiff body, in her movements. You must believe me, *señor.*"

"I believe you," Talley said soberly.

He finished the cigaret, and they got up. Mrs. Partridge was coming from the creek. "I hope," she said, "you are through with your after-dinner smoke."

"We're through," Talley told her, "and ready to travel."

He gave Felipe some tobacco, and Felipe gave him a slab of bacon, and they set out to the north.

"Why do you always give them tobacco?" she asked. "It is worth more than their food."

"It is something they would have to buy. It takes cash."

"Why not give him the money, then?"

Talley shook his head. "He would be deeply hurt if anyone offered to pay for his hospitality."

She snorted. "I don't see any difference. You pay for it anyway."

"Call it a custom," he suggested.

The sky in the northwest was blackening; the wind from that direction was coming with more force, and there was a raw bite to it. "We may have some weather," he observed.

"I hope we are not caught out in a snowstorm."

"It won't snow, but if the wind turns cold it'll be a blue blazer."

"How about Shelby?"

"When we meet him, delay them. My guess is they'll pass you by if you play innocent, and come for me. When they do, I'll be ready for them."

That night they camped under a big walnut tree. The sky was still black in the northwest, but the wind had not grown stronger or colder. "It'll be touch and go," Talley said as he unloaded the pack mules.

When he came back, she had the coffee on. "I thought I might as well be useful," she said.

"It's about time," he said dryly, and eyed her with speculation for a moment.

They ate parched corn and dried beef and drank her coffee, and it was as good as his. Coyotes sang from the top of the rise on each side of them.

Mrs. Partridge shivered. "I don't like coyotes," she said.

"There are a lot of things about this country you don't like," he noted.

"Do *you* like coyotes?"

"Yes, I like their singing. When they are around, it is like having friends as outposts. They—" He broke off and said sharply, "They're singing tonight—on the hilltops!"

She looked up. "You said—"

"In the face of bad weather," he told her sharply, "they don't sing and they don't sit on the hilltops. They go down in the low places and howl."

"That means—"

He got up, trying to move casually. "Stay where you are and act unconcerned, I'll—"

He didn't finish. Hugh Shelby and Joe Cooper and Ned Hungerford and Jesús walked out of the darkness. Cooper and his men carried rifles; Shelby appeared to be unarmed.

Shelby said with that odd sibilance, "Pick up the packs, men. Cooper, keep your rifle on these two. Talley, back up to me slow, with your hands up."

Talley began to turn. The two men picked up four of the saddlebags of quinine and started into the darkness with them. Talley heard a horse whinny. He was still turning.

"Watch that woman!" Shelby ordered. "She's a snake!"

It left Talley uncovered for an instant. He spun faster and kept going around. With his fist doubled, he clubbed Shelby on the side of the head, then leaped free and reached for his pistol.

Cooper turned, and as he did, Mrs. Partridge pulled out her .38 and shot him in the back. The bullet went through his chest cavity and came out the front side, leaving a hole as big as a man's fist, and spraying blood over Talley's hands and face.

At the sound of the shot, Hungerford and Jesús dropped the saddlebags and reached for their pistols. Shelby, staggering, clinched with Talley. He was a big man and powerful. Talley wrestled with him, and twisted him back over Cooper's body. Hungerford fired at him, and Talley, regaining his balance, twisted, drew his six-shooter, and shot the man twice in the abdomen. Hungerford doubled over and fell on his side. Jesús turned and ran, leaving the saddlebags.

Now Shelby was coming at Talley. Talley crashed the pistol barrel over his head, but Shelby grappled with him. He broke loose, pushing Shelby back. Shelby roared forward. He was harder to stop than an Apache—a tougher man than Talley had supposed. Talley brought up the .41 and pulled the trigger. He saw Shelby jerk as the bullet hit him. Shelby's clothes blazed up in fire from the muzzle blast. But Shelby came on against him, and now from somewhere he had a pistol, but Talley shot it out of his hand, and Shelby piled up at his feet, his clothes still burning.

"Put the fire out!" screamed Mrs. Partridge.

Talley shook his head. "He's dead. That bullet got him square in the heart."

They now had three corpses. Talley went after the *bayo*. He rode the horse back to their camp, and saw a strange sight: Mrs. Partridge sitting by the body of Hugh Shelby, weeping silently. Had Mrs. Partridge been in love with Shelby? Perhaps nobody knew or would ever know, but now Shelby was dead, and Mrs. Partridge was crying.

He went around the fire and tied a rope to the feet of Hungerford and hauled him far enough away so they would not be bothered by scavengers. When he returned to the fire, Mrs. Partridge was sitting by the coffeepot, quiet. Her eyes showed no signs of tears. Talley dragged Cooper away, and then Shelby. He glanced at her as Shelby's body was dragged along behind the horse, but she did not look up. He took the bridle off of the *bayo* and walked back to the fire.

"That's good shooting," he said, pouring himself some coffee, for suddenly he felt terribly dry. "Have you reloaded?"

She looked up. "No. I fired only one shot."

He took out his own pistol and filled all the chambers but one. He closed the loading gate, pulled the trigger back to half cock, and spun the cylinder into position. Then, holding the .41 aimed at Mrs. Partridge, he said quietly, "Give me the .38, Mrs. Partridge, and don't make a false move."

She said, "I'll be unprotected."

"You still have me," he said dryly. "Come on. Out with the .38."

She said, "I believe you would shoot me for it."

He answered, "You believe right."

Slowly she pulled it out of the sash at her waist. Her eyes were locked on his, but he did not give her a chance to put her finger on the trigger. Finally she shrugged and held it to him, butt first. He took it and backed away about ten feet. Then he walked into the dark and watched her sit there. He thought she would go looking for Cooper's pistol, but she didn't. He had picked it up when she wasn't looking, but she did not seem further concerned about firearms. He took all four of the pistols that did not belong to him, and pushed them deep into the mud, barrel first, along the edge of the creek. Then he went back to the fire.

"Mrs. Partridge," he said, "we are about home. I advise you not to try anything."

She looked up with a wry smile. "What could I try now?"

"If I knew of anything," he said, "I wouldn't tell you."

The next morning she offered to fry some bacon while he rounded up the animals. "As long as I am reduced to the status of a neutral," she said, "I might as well be useful."

"Suit yourself," he said shortly. He wondered if he had maybe misjudged her a little. He had expected her to sulk.

He brought up the *bayo* and herded the animals to water, then back to the fire. He threw on the packsaddles and the riding saddles, and put the saddlebags in place. Then he turned to the fire.

"I made some corn cakes," she said. "I hope you like them."

Certainly this was a new side to the woman. "I didn't know you could cook," he answered.

"I'm not very good at it. I've never had to be."

He ate the cakes, and they were as good as his own. She got his tin cup from his saddle horn and took it down to the stream to wash it. She came back and filled it with coffee from the can. He sat back against the tree with his fingers laced around the cup waiting for it to cool. "I guess our norther has blown over," he said.

She nodded, sipping her coffee.

He saw then that he had sat in the way of a column of ants that came from beyond the tree to the blood, now dry, that had drained from Cooper's body. He tried his coffee but it was still too hot. He lowered the cup, automatically hunting for his knees with his elbow, but, as before, his knee was higher than he anticipated. His elbow hit it and the jerk spilled a little of the coffee in the path of the ants. In his new position, he propped up his elbows on his knees and tasted the coffee again. "It's good," he said, "but it sure is bitter."

Then he looked down at the ground. First he frowned. Then his eyes widened as he watched the ants between his feet.

She noticed him and asked abruptly, "What's the matter?"

He looked up. "The ants died," he said harshly. "They died quick," and threw the coffee, cup and all, into the fire.

For an instant he listened to the sizzle, and that instant almost cost him his life, for Mrs. Partridge had a hideout gun. She pulled a .31 derringer, with a stub barrel, from the bosom of her dress, and pointed it at him.

But she wasn't fast enough. He drew the .41 and shot her between the eyes. She fell over backward, the derringer still tight in her hand. He watched her long enough to be sure she wasn't faking. Then he took the pistol out of her hand and walked down to the creek. It was getting to be quite a collection of hardware down there in the mud. He went back to the fire and considered her body. He had said once he would turn over only the body of someone for whom he had respect. But after all, she was a woman. He compromised by laying a blanket over her face.

It was early in the afternoon when he pulled his train into Austin. He sat the *bayo* in the street and sent Eph to fetch Captain Robertson. When the gray-uniformed captain arrived, Talley said, "Captain, I've got three thousand ounces of quinine in these bags. Do you want it for the Confederacy?"

"Yes, of course! By all means."

"You can have it for what it cost in Monterrey, plus fifty dollars for my time in running it across the border."

"That's generous of you, Mr. Talley." Robertson looked around. "Didn't Mrs. Partridge—"

"We were—held up," Talley said, "by outlaws who seemed to know exactly what we had. In the fight, Mrs. Partridge was killed."

Captain Robertson took a deep breath. "I'm glad to hear—she died—honorably," he said.

Talley nodded. The lines in the captain's face

were very deep. Talley said quickly, "You want to take delivery of this stuff now?"

"Yes, I will. The sergeant can give us a hand."

They carried the quinine up to Robertson's office, and Robertson gave him a receipt for all except one ounce, which Talley kept. Talley got his animals under way and took them to the Garrisons'. There were two rigs tied in front of the Garrisons', and one looked like Doc Kenedy's. Talley went to the back door and knocked.

The door was opened by Mrs. Kenedy. She said soberly, "Come in, Roy."

He walked in.

Adele met him, her eyes red. "Did you bring the quinine?"

"Sure."

Kenedy came out of the bedroom and he glanced at the paper packet Roy held out. "Is that quinine?"

"Yes," Roy said as steadily as he could. "Is it too late?"

Kenedy took the packet. "Probably not—with this." He went back to the bedroom, then stuck his head out. "Get me a glass of water and a spoon, Adele."

She gave them to him and came back to Roy.

"How long has she been here?" he asked.

"About a week. I rode out to see how she was getting along, and she needed care, so I brought her in."

The doctor came out. "Look for her to turn better by morning," he told Adele. "Keep her warm. She's due for another spell of chills in about two hours, but I'll drop by before then."

After he and his wife had left, with the Reverend talking low-voiced to Mrs. Hancock in the parlor, Talley went to the kitchen with Adele. She poured him some coffee, and he drank it gratefully.

"Mr. Shelby reported in the paper that you had gone to Mexico with Mrs. Partridge," she said. "It was quite a scandal around Austin."

"Hugh Shelby was pretty well informed," he observed.

"You did go with her, though. The whole town saw you."

"I did," he said. "It was to do with the war."

"Did she come back with you?"

"Part way."

She stood before him and looked him in the eye. "Roy Talley," she said, "whatever you did, I want no evasions."

He got to his feet and pushed his hat back on his head. He said, taking her in his arms, "There will be no evasions." He kissed her hard, and there was no evasion on either side.

Center Point Publishing
600 Brooks Road • PO Box 1
Thorndike ME 04986-0001 USA

(207) 568-3717

US & Canada:
1 800 929-9108
www.centerpointlargeprint.com